THE WORLD BELOW

Natalie L. Morris

To my mother,
who will always support me and my
dreams

PROLOGUE

A desk, located inside a small office, which was accessed from a long, narrow hallway. This particular office was nearly bare, containing only the desk and a chair behind it, with two additional chairs facing it. Both of these chairs were occupied. Behind the desk sat a tall, statuesque man, his face hidden beneath a heavy black hooded robe that draped over his entire body. He exudes a serious aura, dominating the room with his presence. The two others seated across from him, waited anxiously for their instructions.

"I have a task that I need you to complete," he stated calmly, his hands folded atop the desk.

"And this task is?" interrupted a teenage boy, his expression somewhat bored.

"You are to join this girl on her journey to the Above," the man replied grimly, setting a photo of a young woman down on his desk. The two teenagers, although they tried their best to mask it, looked slightly surprised when they glanced down, as though they might have recognized the girl in the photograph.

The intimidating man continued, "You must find the entrance together, but you will not let her succeed in traveling beyond that point. This is your task, and afterward, report back to me when the job is complete."

The other person in the room, a girl, asked hesitantly, "What if she refuses to cooperate?"

"That will be up to her—and to both of you. I advise you to be as accommodating and generous as possible to win her over."

He paused, and then added, "Additionally, I will supply you both with weapons for the journey in case of any...threats you might encounter along the way."

The man continued in a hushed voice without any further interruption. After being entrusted with the new assignment, the two teenagers understood what was required of them.

They would follow through with it.

No matter what.

PART 1

CHAPTER 1

Julia

For anyone else the day was beginning like any other. The hallways on the residential levels were currently silent and unoccupied. The only noise was the gentle hum of the air moving through the ductwork that criss crossed our community. A majority of the population were likely still asleep in their own apartments. However, in my small bedroom, I was wide awake and not feeling any remorse for being productive ahead of the morning bell. You could say, this was my favorite time of day. Knowing that I could be alone with my thoughts was a special privilege I granted myself, although I had to do so discreetly. This usually meant spending time creating a world outside my bedroom walls, a place that existed only in my imagination. Sometimes I even allowed myself to wonder if I was alone in these thought experiments. Am I the only one who can see life beyond our existence? Questions such as these have swirled in my head since I graduated from primary school. I have been repeatedly discouraged by the adults in my life from examining or questioning, and instead have been urged to become a "focused member of society." "Focused member?" Is that what becoming one of them means? Is that what it means to become an adult?

Luckily, this morning my curiosities were contained to the world around me. I was focused on preparing for my favorite day of the year.

I sat contentedly on my single bed. A single bed, since I'm still officially single—as in, unmarried. But I'm open to the idea for sure! I definitely have some ideas on that, and his name is always in the back of my mind.

"*Stay focused!*" I mentally reminded myself.

But boy oh boy, is that boy the ultimate distraction. Yes, these thoughts came burrowing in as I sat busily stringing white threads together and sewing pieces of the cloth to make the final touches to my new dress. I absolutely loved dress-making, and this dress might be my best one yet. He is so going to notice me, and just fall even more in love. Yes, I'm in love, and tomorrow, I would wear this dress to a great celebration. A celebration where someone from the society would be chosen to venture out to a strange place known as the Above. The Above was known to all as a place where the light would make the land bright all day and shimmer all night. Sometimes I wished I lived up there as it sounded magical and mysterious. Where I lived had absolutely nothing magical about it, but perhaps there was an element of mystery to be unraveled if one were to look closely.

My home was called the Underground, and its location was, well, underground! You may be wondering, how is this possible? How far underground? Well, this falls in the "mysterious" category as these answers aren't known to the common citizen. All we know, or are allowed to know, is that the lights work, there's an available, unthreatened water source, and enough provided food for the community to thrive. Being underground meant that there is no natural light, or "sunlight" as it's called outside of the Underground. Our sources of light are artificial, meaning our light comes from fluorescent bulbs on our ceilings, or the lanterns that we carry around in the darker recesses of the community.

My room was currently dimly lit by one such lantern and it was just enough light to fight off the darkening shadows that appeared as I worked, as well as the shadows that I tried to keep out of my mind. Swiftly and smoothly, my hands remained steady as I sewed on the final jewels, giving the dress an elevated appearance, fit for such a special occasion. The lantern's glow gave off a warmth that comforted me. I pulled the white crocheted shawl up around my shoulders to fight off the Underground's constant chill. I imagined the lantern to be a cozy fireplace in the middle of winter. Well, that's what I imagined from books...we don't actually have seasons in the Underground, but books are my doorway to a world of possibility and imagination. Carefully, I held up the masterpiece and admired what I had created.

It was a sleeveless dress with a scoop neckline and I made it to be knee length, as was the community policy. A white ribbon cinched the waist just slightly, wrapping around to form a cute little bow in the back. The white ribbon was adorned with tiny little diamonds spread out evenly that sparkled in the glow of the lantern. It was absolutely beautiful.

I was lucky enough to have been taught how to sew from my grandmother. It was her gift to me when I turned 7 years old. She just happened to work as a tailor and helped sew much of the apparel issued throughout the community. Sadly, she's no longer with us but I have the fondest memories of her. She is my dad's mom and had lived a few apartments down the hall from us. She had a zest for life and always looked on the bright side; a glass half full kind of person. She was a kind soul with a nurturing spirit and not a mean bone in her body. She had a gift with people, and a gift for sewing and I love that she passed both of these attributes down to me.

She taught me how to be resourceful and tactful as well, and this has proven useful. For instance, I gather all of my fabric by collecting scraps from the tailoring department before they're discarded into the furnace. From what I find, I'm able to make my own designs. I even help out some of my friends so that they have more unique styles as well.

"What are you doing in there, Jules?" a sleepy voice

came from the doorway, startling me.

"Oh, hi Dad!" I responded cheerfully, "I'm so sorry. Did I disturb you with my light? I was just finishing my new dress. What do you think of it?"

"I got up a little earlier than normal because I needed to run a logistics report at the greenhouse today. Have you really finished? Let me see it," he said, changing the subject as I handed it off to him. He stared at it for a minute, admiring the details, "This is your best one yet! You're getting really good at making these. Your grandmother would be really proud."

I thanked him and hung the dress back in my wardrobe. My dad yawned while watching me tidy up and encouraged me to go back to bed since it was so early in the morning. Without arguing, and fully realizing I had been caught, I turned off the lantern by flicking the on switch to off and climbed into my bed.

"I'm about to head out, but I'll see you later, Jules," my father whispered, kissing my cheek.

"See you," I whispered back to him with a smile on my face.

After he walked out of the room and closed the door, my mind began to wander. The dress I just made was for the biggest event in the community, which only happened once a year. It was always so fun and joyful to see everyone in the community come together, having the time of their lives. But I could feel nerves creeping in at the realization that this year, for the first time, I was of age to be chosen. If I was chosen...I would have to leave the society and everyone and everything I ever knew behind. I might never return! No one who was chosen in past years has returned. Not that I know of, at least. The event, although exciting and well celebrated, also had an overall nervous energy as no one knew who would be next. This year the thought filled me with more dread and anxiety than before. I guess daydreaming over alternate universes and hypothetically imagining a life elsewhere becomes a scary scenario if it were to become the reality. Hopefully, this year I could avoid this fearful unknown and celebrate this special occasion in ignorant bliss.

This special occasion was called The Selection.

CHAPTER 2

Jack

I had awoken earlier than usual as my ever-present worrying thoughts prevented me from falling back to sleep. I tossed and turned all night, unable to rest comfortably. My bed creaked under my weight as I shifted back and forth. I reached over to find the warmth I so desperately needed, but the place was unoccupied. Only the coolness of the empty space remained. My wife, my closest friend, my confidant, my everything. She was gone. She was taken from me ahead of her time. We were supposed to stand side by side and leave this place together, hand in hand. Life unraveled, destroying that plan, and it instead threw us a curveball.

I spent the last few days of her life by her bedside, holding her hand, wiping the tears from both of our eyes, and reading to her as she drifted to sleep throughout the day. Nights were harder for her. She would have night terrors and wake up shaking in fear, hysterical, and inconsolable. I would hold her in my arms as tightly as I could and try to comfort her frail, diminishing body. I discovered if I hummed to her softly, the same tune I had heard myself as a child, this tune would finally bring her peace. I would always try to be there first thing when she woke in the morning and we would have breakfast together, as I would also try to encourage her to eat something, anything. She would smile softly at me, her beautiful eyes still shining as she thanked me for loving her every single day. Those beautiful, shining eyes are the same eyes I fell in love with almost 50 years ago.

I had just begun my internship as a librarian. My mentor was very tough on me and had big expectations. He was an older man and there had always been a sense of urgency about him. He was the most impatient man I had ever met and he was never satisfied with my progress, or lack thereof. He was training me to take his position so there was a lot of pressure placed on my shoulders. As a young man, I worked long, hard hours, night and day, eliminating even the slightest hope for any type of social life. My friends all slowly drifted away until it eventually became just a nod of recognition as we passed each other in the hallways.

Sarah though. She was different. She was someone I had always admired and who had always caught my attention anytime she entered a room. I first noticed her in secondary school. She was a slender, petite girl with thick flowing, wavy, strawberry blonde hair. Her small rounded nose was lightly speckled with freckles and her mouth, oh her gorgeous mouth. She had perfectly shaped lips outlining the shape of a heart, especially when she would purse them while concentrating. She was quick to smile and her eyes would light up as she found amusement in most things. Those eyes—they would really catch me off guard, especially when she would happen to glance in my direction. They were the brightest of blues, like that of the waters surrounding a deserted island. The waves that would crash against this isolated beach is how it felt for me whenever our paths would cross. I was definitely a believer in love at first sight.

In all the time spent observing her from afar, I never did find the confidence to approach her. She was nothing but confident, exuding intelligence and beauty. Her father was on the Council, which only the highest ranking officials were members of. Her mother was equally stunning and was a strong representative in the Committee, the group who helped set the stage of all day to day activities throughout the community.

My own parents were productive members of society, as is what is to be expected of all citizens within the community. My mother was a seamstress and my father worked the furnace. Both would come home at the end of the day exhausted from a hard day's work. As my mother began to age, it was most evident by her hands and the stiffness they would endure. She would ask my father every evening to hold them and massage them. My father was an especially strong and stout man. His strength is what helped him endure feeding the ever hungry furnace that helped fuel the community. His body also began to show signs of aging and he would ache. The pain he would feel in his back would send him to the infirmary regularly, even though they were not able to offer him much support. I would take his place in these instances, trying to relieve some of the burdens he faced. He would take a brief respite and then return to his duties. Both of my parents were proud of me, if not probably a little apprehensive when it came to my shortcomings.

I was more of an introvert to be sure. I would burrow into my small bedroom with a stack of books beside me at all times. The library while growing up only offered a specific genre of literature and this did not fuel the fire for the knowledge that grew within me year over year as I became older. The librarian at the time took note of this and invited me to a special backroom. I am forever thankful to that librarian for encouraging my desire to learn and to grow. With this newfound access, I became even more isolated, as the backroom became my second home. It was my favorite place in all of the Underground and I longed for it whenever I had to depart.

That being said, there were only certain events of which I would willingly participate, or even attend, and of which were required. Looking back now, I should be appreciative of this requirement because it did force me to interact with the people in my community. My parents definitely encouraged these interactions and wanted me to fit in more, especially amongst my peers.

Of course I could still converse with old school friends and we'd get along well enough, but there was a growing disconnect that pulled me apart from them at the same time. Like my growing mind was not able to be bottled up and contained. I was not able to relate to them the same way anymore. I had experienced so many new, exciting ideas and philosophies one can only obtain through reading. Especially when reading material that was not offered publicly. Part of me always wanted more. I wanted more than what existed in the Underground. My desires to experience beyond the walls that contained me was sometimes too much to bear. I would find myself spending even more time in the backroom, reading, researching, looking for answers.

An unexpected answer did come to me without any warning. An answer to a question that I hadn't yet even realized needed to be asked. This changed my life for the better. It forced me to grow in more ways imaginable. It was truly the beginning of life as I knew it, and it all happened during a special occasion.

This special occasion was called The Selection.

CHAPTER 3

Julia

There was an alarm. It rang throughout the entire
community, loud and long. But this wasn't a bad alarm.
It was just the morning bell. It was the same alarm
that would sound at the end of a day announcing that
the shared resources of the community were about to
be closed and that everyone needed to retire to their
apartments. Some of the older residents would reminisce
that a third alarm existed and is still active should the
need arise. Apparently, this alarm was for when the
community needed a warning mechanism for threats
or attacks against the community. I count myself lucky
since I have never heard such an alarm go off or have had
to live in such a potentially scary time.

Startled by this actual morning alarm, I realized
I must have drifted off at some point because the sound
is what woke me. I got out of bed and threw on a white t-
shirt paired with white jeans.

In the Underground, pretty much everyone wore
the same basic fits. For women this included jeans, a
buttoned down top, t-shirts, both short-sleeved and

long, a utilitarian dress, a jogging suit, a down jacket, a watch, a pair of sneakers, and a pair of Mary Janes. One's occupation could alter these but regardless, everyone was issued the same wardrobe to pull from. And every single piece of apparel is white.

Everything in the Underground is white. All of the walls, floors, and ceilings are the same color as well. My bedroom was just that apart from one thing, and it hung from around my neck. I caught my reflection in the mirror and for a moment, I stood there and looked at the necklace, admiring it and relishing what it meant for me to be able to own, wear, and cherish it. I wore it everyday and night. It had a gold rope chain, and a large, rectangular, ruby pendant hung from it. It was the only possession of color I owned and it was uniquely mine to wear.

It had been a gift from my mother. The only belonging of hers I have. See, I don't know who my real parents are because they died when I was very young. All I can remember about my mother is her holding me in her arms, a warm smile on her face, and this very necklace hanging from her neck. Understandably, this necklace is very important to me since it is the only link I have to my past and true identity.

The person I call dad is not my biological father. Since he didn't have any children of his own, he had been approached by the leader of the community and asked if he would be willing to adopt me. I was extraordinarily fortunate to have been raised by such a loving, dedicated, attentive, and supportive father. He even recognizes that he can't possibly take the place of my real parents, but I reassure him that I see him as my dad and nothing will ever change that. I shook my head trying to push these thoughts away and flung on a satchel that held the important tools I would need throughout my workday.

Walking into the kitchen, I noticed that the time was a quarter past 8 and I realized I was running so late! I grabbed a breakfast bar, ran out of our apartment and sprinted to the Grand Staircase. Running past stragglers on the stairs I flew down two levels, in the process joining a large crowd who were walking to and from throughout the community. Many were clearly headed off to their various jobs within the different departments which all worked simultaneously, ensuring our lives ran as smoothly as possible. Others consisted of groups of uniformed children being herded by room mothers. Passing through the corridor, I saw my two best friends standing in the spot they normally congregate in the morning while waiting for me. It was a small sitting nook off to the side and was consistently unoccupied, making it the perfect meetup spot, and a great location from which we could watch all of the morning activity.

"Hey, June! Leo!" I yelled out enthusiastically to them.

My best friend, June, was a short, clumsy, blonde girl with bangs, and hair that went all the way down her back. She was wearing a cute, little white dress that reached her knees, and yes, it was one of my designs. As always, she greeted me with a huge smile. She was always in a happy mood and was usually smiling, but sometimes that smile would lead to her getting into unwanted trouble. She could be a little mischievous, which I loved about her, and discovered her to be a whole lot of fun. It's actually how we became best friends in the first place.

We didn't actually have any classes in school together and although our paths crossed occasionally throughout the years, we were never technically friends until the 3rd year of secondary school. It was in the middle of lunch period, and I had gotten up briefly to run and use the washroom, leaving my lunchbag wide open. When I returned, I found a silly blonde-headed girl with blue eyes helping herself to the strawberries from my lunch! We have been friends ever since.

Leo, on the other hand, had dark black hair, pale skin, and brown, almost black, piercing eyes that would make you feel like he could stare straight through you, into your soul. He was a little bit taller than me, and very fit with a muscular but lean build. He looked more calm than not, and was definitely a bit of a recluse. He tended to be pretty casual and friendly with everyone, but was hesitant to get to know anyone beyond a superficial level and did not seek out making new connections or friendships.

"Hey, Jules!" June replied jubilantly with a great, big smile on her face, as always. "Leo has a pretty busy schedule today. He has to set up for the Selection tomorrow, but I don't have anything planned. Would you mind if I come to the library with you?"

"Of course you can come," I responded, "Although, my schedule today isn't that special. I have to log some time in the back room so I won't be able to hang out very much this morning."

"I'm sorry I can't be with you today, babe," Leo reassuringly apologized, chiming in while kissing the top of my head. Yes, the two of us are dating, and it drives June a little crazy. June and I have been friends a lot longer and having a new boy always hanging around has been an adjustment...probably for both of them. Leo would never have even considered befriending June had she not already been an important part of my life. I think I may be the only thing that they have in common with each other. They've developed a humorous tolerance of being in each other's company that has blossomed into what I think is now sincere. I'm not always so sure because they still argue quite a lot, making me the middleman to tear them apart.

That being said, we all needed to get a move on as our jobs awaited.

Upon graduating from secondary school, all students need to choose from one of the multitude of available jobs offered in the Underground. Most kids tended to follow in their parents footsteps and would end up in the same field as either their mother or father. My friends had chosen positions that were unique to their personalities. June signed up to be part of the Committee, which helped to organize and run all the individual parts of the Underground. She's very outgoing, so it's quite a fitting occupation. She loves getting to know everyone and listening to suggestions to present to the Committee. Her father is actually a member of the Council and her mother is kind of a socialite and spends most of her time in leisure with the other executive wives. Leo's parents, on the other hand, are both teachers. His father is a secondary school math teacher and his mother is a primary school teacher. Leo had joined the maintenance crew. I think he liked to be mostly by himself and to work on well defined physical tasks. This year his crew were responsible for setting up for the Selection.

Unlike most people in our society, I had been chosen to fill a specific, and prestigious job. I am a librarian. I'm not entirely sure how they came to that decision. Out of all the kids in my class, why was I the right person for the job? Regardless, I can't complain. I absolutely love it. I get access to all of the books housed in the entire community, most of which are only accessible to the librarians. Although this job wouldn't seem like it should be prestigious, or even important at all, it has a not so well known function. This function makes it arguably one of the most vital roles in the entire Underground. I am one of only two junior librarians. We have both been trained by and report to the Head Librarian. Between us, I am the newest and by far the youngest. My passion for reading is well known throughout the community so it was an honor to be recruited for this position.

"Ok, this is my stop," Leo announced as the three of us arrived at the gateway to the Great Hall, where the Selection would take place.

"Bye, then!" I replied, wrapping my arms around his neck. He happily accepted this embrace and whispered in my ear, "I love how you always smell like vanilla."

After causing me to blush, we waved bye to each other and June and I continued on our way. Walking beyond the gateway we passed the infirmary, cafeteria, a lounge, and the gym. This corridor was the main hub for the community. Just beyond we took a right, and approached an unimposing single elevator.

Prompting the call for the elevator, the doors opened immediately. Once we stepped in, I pressed the button for the lowest floor in the community. Floor -9. While we rode down, the floor selection buttons blinked in succession, illuminating each floor as we passed through. The -5th floor, from which June and I had just departed, was the main shared space for the community. It had a large central meeting square off of which the staircase is accessed. Branching off from the square were all of the main public functions for the community. The -6th floor was for leadership and executive housing. Only the families of members of the Council and community leaders resided on this level. The next floor down contained workshops, maintenance, tailoring, laundry, and other community services. The -8th floor contained all of the machinery including the electricity generator, water treatment, garbage and sanitation, as well as the furnace. Lastly, the bottom floor, which is where we are headed, has all of the administrative offices as well as my favorite place in the community, the library.

It took only a matter of minutes to make it from the main floor to where I work. When the doors opened, we were presented with the same hallway that I see every day; white walls, fluorescent lighting, and a subtle scent of mold and soap. Today was abnormal in that there was also the Head Librarian, my boss, standing directly in front of us, cradling a book in his arms.

The Head Librarian was an older man who looked as though he was a permanent fixture to the Underground. His thinning gray hair was neatly combed back, though a few strands have now fallen forward, resting against his deeply lined forehead. He wears small, rounded glasses that perch low on his nose, allowing his sharp, intelligent eyes to scan June and I over the top of his frames. His face is etched with the marks of age and countless years spent in quiet contemplation, his expression usually calm and thoughtful. His shoulders tended to slightly hunch, most certainly from the decades of leaning over books and shelves, yet his movements were surprisingly steady and purposeful. His hands, though veined and weathered, always handled each book with the care of someone who has spent a lifetime cherishing the written word. He knew every minute detail concerning the society, and he was trusted greatly by the Council. Yet, somehow, no one knew what his actual name was. He had no living family, and everyone else just called him 'sir'. Personally, I found this to be rather bizarre. There had to be some record that held his name, yet it was never discussed or questioned.

"How are you, sir?" I asked respectfully.

"I am very well, Ms. Brown," he responded, "Thank you very much for asking. Are you ready for the big day tomorrow? I know it's the first Selection for you since becoming a librarian."

"Oh, I'm doing just fine, thank you," I said.

"Well, I can't wait to see you at the celebration. Please be sure to keep up on your...studies," his eyes lingering on the hatchet which hung from my satchel. Then, as if satisfied with the extent of the exchange, he continued with an abrupt, "Farewell" and walked away.

After the Head Librarian entered the elevator and the doors closed behind him, June turned to me and said, "That guy is super weird. Why does the Underground trust him to the extent that they do?"

"Well, he's been here as the Head Librarian for an incredibly long time," I answered, "And he has a ton of knowledge. But I do understand why you would think he is weird. He is eccentric and mostly stays to himself."

As true as that was, it did dawn on me that his pause before saying studies, was also weird. He knows how much time I log in training and has seen my progress reports.

June couldn't help herself and interrupted my thoughts by shrugging and throwing out a, "Whatever you say."

We continued walking to the end of the long hallway, with a row of doors on either side that separated the different department heads' offices. It was by no means glamorous, even though this floor housed the most prestigious positions within the community. Even my boss had an office along this very hallway. Needless to say, the only way someone works on this floor is by holding a high-ranking position, like a society leader or a Council member who makes crucial decisions for the community.

I have only been invited inside the Head Librarian's actual office once and it was the very first day when I was chosen to report to the position. My graduating class from secondary school had just wrapped up the commencement ceremony and we had all proceeded to the school auditorium. Sign up sheets were laid out with delegates from each department welcoming and explaining the various jobs to prospective students. I was wandering around, initially watching from a distance. I considered choosing the gardens because my father worked there. I was about to head in that direction when I was approached by a messenger who handed me an envelope with my name elegantly written in calligraphy on the front. I eagerly opened this mysterious letter to find that the Head Librarian had invited me to become the newest member of this very tight knit group. I couldn't believe it! I was aware that one of the previous librarians, a middle aged man, had just passed away unexpectedly, leaving a position open that could not be left vacant for very long. My dream had always been of working as a librarian, given my love of reading, but I never would have thought that this position would fall to me. I was overjoyed!

The next day I reported promptly to his office on the bottom floor. I knocked on the door and was invited in. For some reason I had been expecting a lavish office filled with old books and a comfortable chair for reading, as I had just assumed that the leaders would have access to such luxuries. Instead his office looked just like all the others; white, bland, and bare. The only difference I immediately noticed was an additional door beyond the desk. The Head Librarian awkwardly flashed me a smile while shaking my hand vigorously. I was surprised at the strength he possessed. He directed me toward the second door and we passed through together into an area of the Underground few had ever seen.

Beyond this ordinary, insignificant office, was the most spectacular room I had ever encountered. It was

a secret library. At least, that's what I like to call it.
The secret library was a grand, quiet space, filled with
towering shelves that held dusty, leather-bound books.
The air smelled of aged paper, and for some reason the
sweet scent of vanilla also overcame me. The glow of
soft lighting from table lamps filled the room and faded
colorful woven rugs covered the floor where we stood.
The atmosphere was one of calm and timelessness, as if
the walls themselves held the stories of centuries. The
space felt like a sanctuary of knowledge, where every
corner invited exploration and contemplation.

Taking in the beauty of the space, I was motioned
to continue over to a sitting area where two small
leather couches faced each other. We sat down and he
began to speak. He told me about how this area held
the oldest books in the entire Underground and that
only the librarians were allowed inside. He handed me
a special key so that I could come and go as I pleased.
He also outlined all of the special training I would need
to complete over the next year so that I could fulfill my
new role. My head was swimming as I tried to process
all of the new information. I tried my absolute best to
remember everything he outlined and promised myself
that I would pour everything into this new endeavor.

"We're here Julia," June's voice startled me back
from my memory.

We had reached the end of the hallway and had
arrived at a door with a nameplate on it that said

"LIBRARY". June and I entered, and we were greeted by a familiar little space filled with the committee approved books on rows of narrow bookcases. Sadly, these book jackets were all in white, yet again, and the room was very stark and sterile in design. I supposed it helped a little that spread around the room were large bean-bag chairs and small, single desks for reading. On the floor was a great, big shaggy carpet that was meant for when the children of the society came into the library during their class time. I've been coming to the library since before I can even remember. Apart from an occasional influx of new reading material, the library has remained essentially unchanged. Almost every one of the books were based upon the Underground itself. Whether it was historical, biographical, fables, or a blend of all three. June lazily picked up a book from the nonfiction shelf, and slumped down in one of the bean-bags. Guess she was settled in for the rest of the morning.

Looking around the room, I sighed. I had a lot of things to do in preparation for the Selection. The room itself was in order, but I knew what was falling on my shoulders for the upcoming event. Even though it wouldn't be expected from anyone else in the community, the librarians had three main responsibilities:

1. Ensuring the safety of the people.
2. Maintaining a repository of knowledge that could be called upon in the face of a challenge.

3. Providing a source of strength and courage in the case of an attack from outsiders.

Because of this, the librarians needed to receive special training, and overtime, became expert combatants. This was an extra skill set I had worked diligently to master and had to consistently keep up on my practice log sheets. It is very important that we are as well prepared as possible for the worst case scenario.

I've read that time is fleeting, and also that time is of the essence. In a book written by a man named William Shakespeare, he states that "parting is such sweet sorrow." From these insights, I've come to realize that there will never be enough time to accomplish everything that needs to be done.

Always more to learn, never enough time.

CHAPTER 4

Jack

A loud alarm echoed throughout the Underground, the community's morning wake-up call, signaling the start of another day. Sitting up and beginning to stand, I stretched my ever aging body, waking up every body part that fought to stay at rest. I proceeded to turn on some accent lighting, just to fight off the complete darkness that would otherwise exist. With every switch the cool chill that existed throughout the rooms lightened, and the unique space that I called home could be fully appreciated.

I have to give all of the credit to my wife. She was special that way, and with her connections, or just plain wit, she somehow managed to obtain any object she desired. We lived in a more secluded part of the community and with that came a few more privileges, but also some challenges which forced me out of my comfort zone. Our shared apartment was ours, and ours alone, and few were ever welcomed into our little secret abode. Fear of being discovered kept everyone at arm's length. We were happiest this way and having each other to come home to at the end of the day was enough to keep us content.

Continuing into the living room, I switched on the last remaining light and it cast off a colorful depiction of shadows on the white walls behind it. My wife had become a bit of an art historian, or more like a collector of fine things. That this directly opposed community policy was not lost on me. My wife broke the mold in so many ways and I didn't even attempt to restrain her creativity, in fact I encouraged it. I suppose I am partially to blame for nurturing this creative, beautiful soul as she grew into the person she was always meant to be. My little shining star.

Straightening up as I walked through the room, I allowed myself to admire all of the beauty that adorned every nook and cranny. My wife's influence was in every single decision and every object that occupied the space. A Persian rug, now faded in its rich colors of burgundy, greens, and blues, still soft under my bare feet, was the focal point of the room and it kept the room grounded, preventing it from floating away...even if that was probably what she had wanted all along. A velvet blue lovechair centered the room. Directly in front, a rectangular cocktail table, its legs short and delicate in design. The finish was faded and had patinated with age. Two wingback accent chairs, with matching striped upholstery bringing out the ivory and blue accents from the rug, sat lovingly on either side of the loveseat.

A floor to ceiling bookcase flanked the entire back wall. It had become an accumulation of what the two of us enjoyed discovering throughout the years. Most were explorations of far flung corners of the globe, as we both ached to see and explore the wonders of the world outside of the Underground. Many of hers had to do with art: Modern art, abstract art, contemporary, photography. She relished in them all and absolutely loved staring at the images that popped from every page as she slowly studied them, taking in the tiniest of detail with her gifted eye. We had both acquired various cookbooks over the years and dreamed of what different foods and flavors might actually taste like. Not having access to all of the necessary ingredients made it impossible to prepare. Imagining the dishes became a pastime we shared together.

A small secretary desk was placed against the front wall, and this is where she did most of her writing. She kept a journal, and it contained her most inner thoughts, fears, concerns, and dreams. The drawers of the desk were filled with the many previous volumes she had poured herself into over the years we had shared together. Fresh flowers would routinely be placed in a simple vase that rested atop the mahogany finished wood. Her favorite flowers were daisies, which was fitting as she wanted the essence of joy to spill into any room she occupied.

The walls were a gallery of the most beautiful

landscapes. One could get lost into the images depicted in the ornate golden frames. The one that centered directly behind the loveseat was by far the largest, and the most eye-catching. It was magical. I am sure it was where my wife longed to spend her days. The painting was one of an enchanted garden. The sky was the perfect shades of blue and pink, with puffy clouds of white, gray, and yellow. The sun was shining in between these clouds, casting down its brilliant rays into the garden. Giant evergreen trees filtered this light as it descended further into the garden, shadows darkening the scene below. At the base of the garden, amongst these surely pine scented trees, was a small grass filled meadow. The stillness of the meadow only accentuated the beauty and differed from the swaying feel of the wind blown branches that hung directly above. Flowers flanked on all sides filling the picture with additional colors and accenting the beauty and uniqueness each flower brought to the canvas. Amongst the trees, a single weeping willow bore the full extent of the sun. Its branches also caught the wind as it was lifting away from the scene. The majestic willow brought an air of sadness and a longing for something undefined to anyone who was lucky enough to study it. In the middle of the meadow sat a young lady whose face was turned away. She was wearing a pale blue Victorian dress with white lace and trim, and she was seated on a blanket strewn carefully beneath her. My wife often fantasized that she was this woman. Wearing such a frock amongst nature and soaking up every bit of her surroundings. The colors, the scents, the sounds. Sadly, I was never able to make this dream come true for her, but I would always try to cheer her up in other ways.

Realizing I had been lingering for far too long, I began to pile up the numerous papers that had scattered across the room. Upon taking over my predecessor's position, I instantly found myself seated at the Council's table. The work was endless, and it monopolized much of my time. More and more of my focus had shifted to the Council and the endless amount of meetings that they insisted I attend. The upcoming Selection was more contentious than was typical. You could feel a sense of unease coursing through the group. Normally the Council welcomed my guidance, but this time there seemed to be a resistance to accepting my proposals. They were fixated on all the wrong things, misinformed fears that became truths in their minds. It was becoming a losing battle. A lost cause and I knew I was going to have to change tactics.

Never enough time.

CHAPTER 5

Jack

I headed straight to my office. I had spent enough time squirreling away in my apartment. Off of the executive level of residences there is a more private way to move throughout the community. Walking up to it now, I pushed the button, calling for the elevator. The doors immediately opened, as if awaiting my arrival. I punched -9, taking me to the lowest level within the Underground. My office was located on this level amongst the other administrative offices that resided on this floor. Nothing about the hallway suggested any semblance of authority, as most spaces in the community were designed to remain white and nondescript by nature.

Upon reaching my office door, I began to search for the one key I needed, amongst an entire ring full of keys. Finally finding the correct one, I unlocked the door and ducked inside. Usually, I don't run into anyone in this particular hallway. Most people don't actually use or work out of their designated office space. I am unusual in this regard, and it suits me just perfectly that the floor remains mostly unoccupied. The library is adjacent to my office so the only noises that periodically arise are the small voices of children and women who congregate while visiting the library during their school day. Sadly, other colleagues do know that they can usually find me in one of these spaces so they are able to track me down and force me to face them directly. Avoiding these interactions, or lately, altercations, has become something that I have to work at to actually be successful. Thankfully, having keys and access to spaces others don't has been a saving grace.

I had specifically come in search of one particular book I hadn't been able to get out of my mind. It was a book littered with figurative language and a storyline that emphasized the importance of strategy and leadership, both of which I was desperate to get a better handle on. Leaving my sham of an office, I proceeded through another door which opened into a private library. This library was my true office, my true oasis, my true sanctuary. The books found here were a priceless collection, stored and protected ever since the creation of the Underground.

I was very selective about whom I recruited to trust and share this library with, carefully considering the role and responsibilities that being a librarian entails. I have yet to find my true successor, but my latest recruit shows qualities I recognized in myself at her age: a passion for knowledge, a willingness to learn, and an ability to look beyond our world in search of something more. Naturally, her love of reading was a clear factor. As I watched her grow up, I noted how she interacted with peers, teachers, and other community figures. She has always been someone I kept a close eye on.

I only have two active librarians at a time, so when tragedy hit and I unexpectedly had to nominate a replacement, her name immediately came to mind. Within this selective group I can safely be her mentor, her protector, her advocate.

Strolling through the familiar aisles of books, I finally found the volume I was looking for. I wanted to ensure I was not to be disturbed so I took the book, and grabbed the stack of practice log sheets that had piled up waiting for me to review. I proceeded to lock everything up and headed back to the elevator. Pushing the call button didn't grant me immediate access this time. Seeing the numbers light up and blink above the door I waited as the elevator began its descent from -5.

The doors opened and there stood Julia. Julia and her friend to be more exact. Julia is my most recent recruit and she is the one who I have always had a watchful eye over. In addition to myself, the Council has also shown interest in Julia as she has grown throughout the years. It is rare in the community for someone to be so unfortunate as to lose both of their parents at such a young age. Looking at her now, it dawns on me that she could just as easily be my granddaughter. My wife and I were not fortunate enough to have a child, although it wasn't for lack of desire.

We were fond of both Julia's birth parents and we, as a couple, had become quite close friends. Her father was rising to prominence in the community and had just become the newest member of the Council when I first had the opportunity to meet him. We instantly connected. His way of thinking was so eerily similar to my own. He was a strong, independent thinker so it was surprising that the Council brought him into the fold to begin with. I myself was excited for a fresh, new perspective. He was also raised by equally thought provoking parents who made big strides in the development of the Underground.

Julia's mother I didn't know as well. I never heard about her earlier years, before she was married, or before they had had a child. She was warm and a great listener and became close friends with Sarah. Sarah loved getting to experience motherhood secondhand through her friend. That was enough for me to accept them as our closest friends. I usually try to relinquish these types of memories because it isn't fair to either Julia or myself. There is no time for that type of casual relationship between the two of us. Early on the Council made the decision that Julia's past remained in the past and therefore hidden from her upbringing. When she was adopted, both my wife and I removed ourselves as prominent figures in her life and instead, kept watch of her from afar.

Julia stepped out of the elevator, politely greeting me. The exchanges between us were always without fault and pleasant enough. Her friend on the other hand I found to be loud and overbearing. Of course it was obvious they were headed to the library. She is the only librarian I can recall who carried a weapon on their person at all times while roaming around the community. I never instructed her to do this, as usually the weapons do not leave the training facility. I allowed this one discretion without drawing any attention to this abnormality.

The community has no weapons and no tolerance for violence of any kind. As far back as anyone in the Underground can remember, we've never had a need for weapons or even a reason to know how to act in violent situations. Yet, as librarians, we are expected to know how to use these tools solely for protection and to be prepared to fight, should the need ever arise.This so-called need was based on fears of the Above. The Counselor, who is our appointed leader, has made sure to impress upon every single citizen the ever present risks we face just existing below their surface. He, as have the Counselors before him, all successfully inflicted fear amongst the community and the people have put all of their trust in Him. He is their protector and defender.

That being said, there is one exception: the senior members of the Council were all given access to a hidden armory which contained weapons, including a collection of firearms from the very beginning of the Underground. These were the only lethal weapons in the entire community, and the rest of the population doesn't even know of its existence. I was issued my key when I became Head Librarian and have not entered that hidden room once since the day I received it.

Preparing to depart from Julia and her friend, I reminded her to stay up on her studies. I want her to be as prepared as possible for the unknown future that is always ahead of us all. I could've never predicted where my life could have possibly taken me when I was her age.

As I entered the elevator, I made a quick decision to do a quick assessment of all of the departments since the Selection was less than 24 hours away.

CHAPTER 6

Julia

The hatchet flew through the air perfectly end over end before striking the mounted target dead center.

I was spending the morning practicing for the Selection, of course. As a librarian, I was trained to protect the people of the society if danger falls upon the great event. The pressure kind of made me nervous, but I would survive. Becoming this skilled had taken a lot of practice, but it was worth it because now I hardly ever miss the bullseye! My weapon of choice was obviously the hatchet, but I just began training with daggers, and once I am proficient in those I will be able to train on other weapons as well.

Walking up to the target, I pulled out my hatchet and secured it in its place on my satchel. Currently, I am in the backroom of the library, which can be entered through a locked door behind the front counter. Unbeknownst to me at the time, this is the same space that I had accessed from the Head Librarian's office. The space is significantly larger than I had first realized as it is actually split into two different areas. Half was the private library and the other half housed the training facility.

My awe of the secret, or private library has not diminished since my first introduction nearly a year ago. This private library stored the books from before the Underground existed. It was almost entirely filled with the works of authors from the Above who had lived many years ago. Books of all genres were shelved here, but the truly special thing about these relics was that they were all different colors. The books themselves each had a differently designed book jacket, and the pages were filled with different fonts, coloring, pictures, etc. Seeing them all displayed in endless rows was a glorious sight to behold. The smell was different in this library as well. It was a very rustic, smoky, vanilla scent, and being amongst these priceless books put me instantly at ease. In my short time as a librarian, I have barely made a dent in consuming all that the library has to offer. But I feel proud of myself for making it my own personal goal to read every single book that is stored here.

This library was a surreal place for me. It filled me with a joy that no one else could compete with. Not my father. Not my friends. Not even my boyfriend could make me as happy as reading did. Reading was an escape from the reality of the world, and a way to exist in a newly constructed universe which only existed in one's own mind and within the story itself. Each story could either put me at ease, filling me with a sense of peace, or rattle me completely with tales of chaos and tragedy. My favorite was a collection of fictional stories about a group of teenagers living in a world where magic existed. I found that these stories could put a smile on my face in some instances, or bring me to tears in the next.

Unexpectedly, I heard a chime from the bell that was stored on the front desk counter. Making sure my satchel was secure, I went through the door entering back into the main library. I saw June patiently waiting for me. My best friend's face lit up with excitement at seeing me come to join her. It always did whenever she saw me, making me feel incredibly special.

"Hey, girl!"June exclaimed joyfully, "I was bored of reading, and I wanted to talk to you. You've been in that backroom forever."

"What time is it?" I asked casually, smiling at her over dramatic nature.

"It's already noon, Julia," June answered, "Let's go grab some lunch in the cafeteria. I'm starving!"

I agreed to her idea, so I locked up the back room and we headed out to catch the elevator back up to the main floor.

Walking into the cafeteria was a small adjustment to my morning, as it was switching from complete silence and concentration, to loud competing conversations and just pure chaos. June thrived in this environment so she was instantly happy to blend into the room. We grabbed a couple of lunch sacks that were pre-packed with a sandwich and an apple and spotted an open table on the far side of the room. Goodness, walking through the maze of chatter and eyes made me feel like I was instantly back in secondary school. June lit up and was greeting everyone as we passed. I smiled and followed patiently behind June until we finally arrived at our table and could sit. I noticed that eyes were still lingering on us as we started to unpack our sacks, but I was trying my best to ignore them. June and I have been best friends for a while so I'm kind of used to the attention that comes with hanging around her. June decided to dive immediately into the most current gossip that was going around, mostly having to do with people we used to go to school with.

Looking around more cautiously than normal, my best friend proceeded to lean in towards me.

"Julia?" she whispered, "I've actually heard some gossip about you."

Slightly alarmed, I asked, "What are they saying?"

"They're calling you a snob," she explained, "They say that ever since you became a librarian, you have been more distant from the rest of the society; like you think that you are superior to the rest of us. They say that before, you always enjoyed talking to everyone in the Underground as much as possible. But after you got this job, well, that's changed. The rumor is that you are no longer a trustworthy member of society."

"What!" I exclaimed. I couldn't believe it! Shaking

my head in disbelief I bellowed out, "That's not true! Who is saying all of these things about me? I love this community and everyone in it! I've just been so busy reading and training that I don't have as much leisure time. It's not like we are in school anymore so this is ridiculous!"

"I suspected that was what was happening," June said leaning back into her chair, "It's okay, Julia. The rumors have definitely stemmed from old classmates. They're all a bunch of meanies, and probably just jealous!"

I smiled a big smile at her, and she gave me a big smile back. A small ding chimed coming from June's general direction, interrupting our conversation.

My best friend was wearing her community issued watch. Everyone in the society wore one, as it was used as a communication device between members of the Underground. She looked down at the watch on her wrist, and her smile instantly disappeared.

"Ugh, Leo wants me to help him with something in the gym for some reason," June said, rolling her eyes, "You know how he is when he's working out."

I just laughed at her and commented, "It's so great you guys have started hanging out more! You think maybe you'll stop fighting so much now?"

I chuckled while giving her a little nudge. Leo, for some odd reason, had just recently begun inviting June to come keep him company while he was exercising. I think he enjoyed having her cheer him on as it made him somewhat more confident. Habitually, I rubbed my own wrist, and then realized something. I didn't have my watch on! I definitely didn't see it in my room at home this morning, so when did I last have it? Thinking back, I remembered taking it off to help my dad in the garden the day before. I must've left it there

"I have to go too, June," I said, beginning to stand up, "I think I left my watch in the garden."

She nodded as we began cleaning up our table. I couldn't help but to feel thankful for having June stick by me even with the gossip swirling around about me. We proceeded to walk out together and take the short walk down the hall to the gym. I gave her a quick hug and let her know that as soon as I grabbed my watch I'd come straight back to join them both. I was really hoping my watch was still in the garden!

Instead of walking back to the tiny, cramped elevator, I decided to take the stairs and began taking them two by two all the way from -5 to the top, -1. The -4th and -3rd floors were primarily general housing. Both of these floors are identically designed. Hallways flanked with identical apartments all stemming from either direction of the Grand Staircase. The only way to tell them apart was to take note of faintly etched numbers and letters distinguishing one hallway and apartment from the next. My father and I live on Floor -3, Hallway 7, Apt. F, while Leo lives on the same floor but a completely different Hallway. The preschool, primary, and secondary schools were all on the -2nd floor. The very top floor housed the Underground's food production with large greenhouses, the farming unit, as well as food processing.

Both the garden and the farm were accessed by passing through multiple sets of double doors. The doors separated the society and this area to maintain a clean and nontoxic environment. They also have a different, more advanced air filtration system, temperature controls, as well as an advanced lighting element to be able to remotely adjust lighting in different areas of the greenhouse. Rows and rows of vegetation lined the majority of the space growing all types of vegetables, herbs, and even fruits. The space is so large that there was even room for seasonal fruit trees and various flowering plants. I entered through the sets of double doors and spotted a group of workers clustered together in the middle of one of these rows. Amongst them my own father stood writing notes on a clipboard.

He had worked at the greenhouse ever since he was young and really enjoyed being a Garden Supervisor. It seemed like he knew everything there was to know about growing and keeping plants healthy. It was what he loved to do.

"Hi Dad!" I shouted out waving to him. All heads turned to look at me, as not many people were allowed into the gardens without permission. As I made my way over to my dad, the others began to whisper quietly to each other, all the while peering in my direction. My father, however, smiled a big, wide smile, and gave me a large hug. He was wearing a white lab coat, but also gloves that were covered with dirt, so when he hugged me, he made sure his hands didn't touch me.

"Hi, Jules!" He said, "What are you doing here?"

"I lost my watch, and I think I may have left it here," I replied looking around.

He took off one of his gloves, and reached into the pocket of his coat, pulling out a watch. My watch!

"I found this when I came in here earlier," he said, "I suspected it was yours, but I wasn't entirely sure."

I thanked him, and put the watch back on my wrist. Suddenly, a woman rather urgently rushed into the garden and frantically called out to my father.

"David!" she yelled, referring to him by his first name, "We need help in the farm unit! A goat got out of its pen!"

"Coming!" my dad shouted back, before turning back to me smirking as he ran in the farm's direction, "I've gotta go, but I'll see you later. Bye sweetheart!"

"Bye Dad!"

After I left the greenhouse, I walked down the staircase back to floor -5. Now that I had my watch back, I was headed straight to the gym. I casually greeted and smiled at other members as I passed by, still replaying the earlier conversation I had had with June. Me, a snob?

Clearly not! Maybe I'm just a little misunderstood...

When I entered the gym, I immediately saw Leo
and June. My best friend was cheering him on while also
idly distracted by her watch. He was lifting weights and
clearly working really hard because he looked pretty
sweaty. Walking over to them, I again noticed a few
people looking at me strangely, but I decided to ignore
them. I received more and more unwanted attention ever
since I became a librarian.

"Hey guys!" I exclaimed, "How's it going in here?"

"I'm just about done. I was actually thinking of
heading home to shower, if you'd like to join?" Leo asked
while throwing me a cheeky smile, raising his eyes to
meet mine as he lowered the dumbbell to the ground.

Before I even had a chance to answer, June
interrupted, "Seriously? Guys, I'm sitting right here! Can
you please try not to do this in front of me?"

Leo and I looked at June, and then back to each other
and burst out laughing. I am so happy we have such a
good sense of humor around each other. As Leo grabbed
his stuff we all started walking back towards the Grand
Staircase and headed for home.

Since June's father is a member of the Council, she
lived in the executive residences one floor down so she
left us on the stairs as we proceeded to go up a couple
more levels. Leo and I walked in silence until we reached
his apartment, stopping in front of the door. He looked
into my eyes, and smiled, and I just smiled back in

response.

Leo lived by himself. When a person in the Underground turns 18, they have the option to get their own place, or continue living with their parents. While June and I chose to stay with our parents, Leo preferred a more private home life. He and his parents came to a crossroads and began arguing constantly. Neither of his parents were supportive of the path he chose in going into the maintenance department. They didn't think it was thought provoking enough and that he was capable of contributing at a higher level. He disagreed and tried to convince them that he enjoys working with his hands, learning how things work, and making repairs. Because of this rift, he made the decision to get his own place. I'm considering getting my own apartment after the Selection, but am feeling conflicted about leaving my dad since we are super close.

My boyfriend leaned down to kiss me, and I reciprocated the gesture. We stood like that for a few seconds, before he parted with me, and said goodbye. After he walked into his apartment, I took a deep breath and continued down the hall towards my own apartment. It was eerily quiet, especially this time of day. Perhaps everyone was still getting ready for the Selection, but that same silence and reasoning made my mind wander again. Particularly about the Selection. What if I was chosen? What if someone I cared about was chosen? How would that cause my life to change?

As I considered all these life altering possibilities, I heard a ding and looked down to read a message on my watch. It was from Leo.

"*I love you.*"

Smiling, I messaged him back, "*I love you too.*"

CHAPTER 7

Jack

The elevator door shut and I quickly selected -8. This was a very familiar level for me. It was my fathers floor. A floor full of hustle and bustle. Within seconds I had arrived and was instantly overwhelmed by the flow of bodies as they busily rushed from one place to the next. I never enjoyed my time spent here and it does bring up some sadness since it also always reminded me of my father. We were never super close, but he was a role model who instilled in me hard work and dedication. More importantly, how to be an amazing husband and loving father. He was always there for me and supported me even when I knew he didn't always understand my hopes and dreams.

There is no one left from his generation on this floor. It is filled with new faces, younger faces and bodies. The furnace room is located at the very far end of the hall and has thick steel doors protecting the rest of the floor from the constant heat it produces. The job is not easy and it is very physically demanding. I would come home covered in grime and sweat, my hands raw with blisters, and an ache that began at my feet and worked its way the entire length of my spine up to my neck. My father was incredibly strong and resilient. He appreciated it when I would step up and take his shifts when he got older and couldn't manage quite as easily. Two men work a shift at a time. One is carting and dumping coal, or picking up trash collection that has been sorted through for the purpose of burn. The other is hauling and feeding it into the mouth of the furnace. The furnace is on a schedule where the fire is fed coals or trash ensuring it is a constant resource. The coal is stockpiled in adjacent rooms. There is a never ending supply as it was all salvaged during the time of building out the Underground centuries ago, as well as the fact that the entire area surrounding the Underground contains more should the need ever arise.

Water treatment, garbage and sanitation, as well as the generator, were also located on this overworked level. My experience with these departments was limited at best. The community had great leadership heads in each of these departments who were experts in their craft and skilled at teaching and retaining the future generations who were to follow behind. This floor was imperative to the success of everyone's day, beginning to end, so a lot of time, dedication, and resources were spent to ensure it ran efficiently, effectively, and as smoothly as possible.

After peeking my head in and nodding to anyone who noticed my presence, I proceeded to take the stairs up to level -7.

This level was much more calming and there was far less male presence. This level was spotless and the purest of white blanketed the space throughout. The tailoring department was a constant hum of quiet activity, and the occasional chatter and giggles could be heard as girls and women completed their work. Large bolts of white fabric, white wool, and white linens were stored in the back room of this space. A large section of cabinets and endless rows of various sized drawers lined the walls storing all of the necessary supplies to successfully sew the pieces of clothing. Half the room was filled with tables running parallel to each other, all used for different purposes while handling the material. The other half, towards the front, was set up more like a classroom setting. It was a grid of workstations, each outfitted with individual sewing machines. These machines would be the background noise throughout the day.

My mother worked in the tailoring department. She was a skilled seamstress, and although it was sometimes tedious work, her favorite part of her role was building friendships with the other women she worked beside every day. She loved these women dearly and they really were like a second family to her. At some point as I grew older, I was less excited about stopping by to visit her. The attention I would receive as a young boy was nothing short of embarrassing. Of course my mother loved every single second of it and could not understand why I would shy away from such positive complimentary attention. They were actually very sweet ladies, to be sure. Oftentimes I would come home to find that my mother had brought me a special, unique piece of clothing that I could add to my wardrobe. I had special pieces like vests or jackets, that no one else would be able to duplicate.

The layout of this level was very smartly designed as nothing was too far from anything else within the community. Jumping from the residential areas down to this level was very doable and work flowed through the departments seamlessly. Laundry was conveniently located on this level, as well as maintenance. The laundry room was another bustling room full of movement and productivity. Upon entering the room the air was definitely warmer, but also rich with the strong smell of soap and detergent. Large industrial washing machines were a constant whirl of movement throughout the day. Just opposite these machines, were equally impressive dryers that could hold multiple loads of clothing at a time. Since everything was white, it was fairly simple to throw everything in together and sort through the ownership labels afterward. Upon exiting the dryers, everything would either be steamed, hung, or ironed. It was a long day for the workers who staffed this area. But yet there was a comfortableness as well. There was no sense of urgency or stress. Everyone knew what was expected of them and everyone just chipped in to complete the orders as they came in. Couriers would come and go as they picked up laundry bags labeled by individual apartments, dropping them off in the soil bins, and at the end of the day run the finished, clean clothing and linens back to the correctly tagged residences.

Lastly, maintenance. This was the other larger department that occupied this level. The training involved in this department was probably a little more time consuming and required learning on the job as things arose. People here were not expected to know much initially. Overtime they would gradually learn how everything worked and eventually could become the community expert on something specific. If something broke, the department would be notified and would send the person most skilled for that particular task to make the repair. It was also a smartly managed department and many of the young men would begin their roles in the community in this area. Maintenance also had an extension area which covered general cleaning as well. While the younger crew was in training oftentimes they would double this with a regular cleaning schedule to ensure everything remained spotless in all of the common areas.

As I did my final lap around the level, continuing to poke my head in and out of all the departments, everything looked as it should and I was content to move on with my day. Glancing down at my watch I caught the time and realized it really was time for me to get to my preparation work that I had to complete before I met with the Council that very evening. This will be the final meeting before the Selection and it is imperative that it goes well.

CHAPTER 8

Julia

"What are you doing?" a voice behind me whispered menacingly. Moments earlier, I had walked into an empty apartment, heading straight to the kitchen to make myself a snack. Just as I reached for something in the pantry, that chilling whisper slid up my spine, making me shiver in fright. My heart skipped a beat as I slowly turned around, pulse racing.

"Dad?" I said, a mixture of shock and disbelief on my face. There he was, my father, standing in the kitchen doorway, trying his hardest to hold back a fit of laughter. I couldn't believe it—I'd fallen for his antics again!

Why am I always so easy to scare?

He kept up the act for another moment, his eyes gleaming mischievously. "I was planning on making your favorite dish for dinner," he said in that same eerie voice.

"Cake?" I asked with a laugh, rolling my eyes, both of us knowing my answer was far from serious. At that, Dad couldn't hold back any longer and burst into laughter, his hearty chuckle filling the room as his eyes teared up with mirth. After a moment, he caught his breath and came over, still smiling as he explained, "Tonight, it's tomato soup. The garden is overflowing with tomatoes, so I thought we'd make the most of it."

I grinned at the thought of fresh tomato soup and nodded enthusiastically. We didn't always get the chance to cook together; our schedules rarely aligned. But tonight was different. Tonight was our night.

I grabbed the stock pot from the cabinet while Dad started gathering the ingredients, placing each one on the counter with a sense of purpose. As we worked in sync, I casually asked, "So, how was the rest of your workday? Did you finally get control of that rowdy goat?"

"Oh goodness, the goat!" he exclaimed with a dramatic sigh. "Well, I thought I was dealing with just one escapee, but it turned out to be the entire herd. One after another, they managed to wiggle their way out of the pen. It was chaos! It took a whole crew of us to round them up. You should have seen it! I should've called you to come help."

I laughed, trying to stifle a grin. "I would've loved to! I like helping you in the garden, and I enjoy learning about how you care for the animals and grow all the food we eat."

Dad paused for a moment, stirring the soup thoughtfully. "How are you finding things at the library, Jules? You know, I had always hoped you would've ended up working in the garden as well. We could've worked side by side, and I could have tormented you there too!"

His eyes twinkled at the idea, and I couldn't help but smile back.

"That sounds...fun?" I replied, chuckling. "But really, I do like being a librarian. It's just more intense and time-consuming than I expected. June even mentioned that people in the community have noticed I'm not as available as before, and they're apparently spreading a few...not-so-flattering rumors about me. If it weren't for that, the job would be perfect."

My dad's face softened, and he gave me a reassuring look. "People can be quick to judge, especially when they don't understand. Librarians have a certain prestige in our community, and with that comes a degree of...well, suspicion. It's just how things are."

I sighed, relieved that he understood. "What should I do about it, Dad? I don't want to end up ostracized."

He placed a comforting hand on my shoulder. "Just be true to yourself, Jules. The right people will recognize that and come to your side in time."

He hesitated for a moment, then continued, "There is something else I wanted to talk to you about, though. Something important."

"What is it?" I asked, sensing a shift in his tone.

"It's about the Selection," he said quietly. The word alone sent a jolt through me. He took a breath, clearly hesitant. "This year, you turned 18, and as you know, everyone over 18 is eligible to be chosen. I want you to be prepared...just in case."

I tried to mask my nervousness, forcing a lighthearted tone. "But there's only a tiny chance I'll be chosen, right?"

Dad's expression was serious, and he nodded slowly. "Yes, but if either of us is chosen, I've come up with a plan. The person who's chosen will leave markers at major junctions along the way, and after a week, the person who remains behind will follow those markers through the tunnels. That way, we can reunite on the other side. We won't have to be separated forever."

I was taken aback by the careful thought he'd put into it. "That's…brilliant, Dad. Then, if one of us does get chosen, we'll find each other, no matter what. And if we make it… we'll both be in the Above."

He smiled, his eyes warm and steady. "You're strong enough, Jules. Strong enough to face anything."

My heart swelled, feeling a surge of love and gratitude. I'd do anything to keep him proud, to hear his laugh, and to feel the warmth of his presence by my side.

"I love you, Dad," I said softly, reaching out to hold his hand.

He squeezed my hand gently, his voice equally tender. "I love you too, Jules."

◆ ◆ ◆

No matter how hard I tried, sleep wouldn't come. I tossed and turned, thinking about what awaited me the next day. My mind was a tangled web of thoughts, refusing to find the peace it needed to finally relax. So, as any normal person would, I decided to go for a walk.

Quietly, I slipped out of the apartment and made my way up the staircase to floor -2, the level that housed the primary and secondary schools. The hallway was silent, its stillness broken only by the soft hum of the lights. Outside the main doorway to the primary school, I paced back and forth, trying to ease the knots in my stomach. I knew what I needed more than anything right now: someone to talk to.

I checked my watch, relieved that I'd remembered to wear it, and sent a quick message to the one person who might be awake at this hour. The night owl who dreaded mornings but thrived long after dark. The mentor who'd always inspired me to keep going, no matter how tough things got.

I messaged Molly, the other librarian, and was surprised when she responded right away, agreeing to meet. A few impatient minutes later, she appeared, her face lighting up with that familiar warm smile. Molly was a middle-aged woman with a cascade of full, curly brown hair that reached just past her shoulders. She wore it differently every time I saw her, but tonight, it was loose and casual. Her t-shirt and shorts matched mine, making it feel like we were meeting in some kind of midnight club. Despite the late hour, she looked bright and awake, as if she belonged to the night.

"Hey, Julia," she greeted me cheerfully, "How are you

on this lovely night?"

I couldn't help but laugh. "I'm...ok, I guess. A little nervous, but ok."

She nodded knowingly. "I know the feeling," she said, still smiling. "The night before my first Selection, I was terrified. I kept imagining every worst-case scenario. But it's natural to feel nervous—it's a big day. Besides, isn't there something a little exciting about it too?"

I gave a half-nod, though I wasn't sure I fully believed it. She might be right, and I might be overreacting, but my gut insisted that something would go wrong.

"It'll be fine," Molly reassured me, pulling me into a gentle hug. "In all the time the Underground has existed, there's never been an attack. The chances that you'll actually need to intervene are incredibly slim. Just try to enjoy the experience, Julia. Do you hear me?"

I managed a small smile. "Yeah," I replied, feeling a bit more at ease. Molly's gaze drifted to the primary school building beside us, and her smile grew even wider, as if a fond memory had taken hold.

"I remember when I was a student here," she said, her voice filled with nostalgia. "On my first day of primary school, I woke up so excited. I was dressed, fed, and out the door in record time. When I arrived, I saw a few familiar faces, which helped calm my nerves. And when the teacher started teaching us the alphabet...well, that was the moment I felt like the whole world was opening up before me."

I chuckled, nodding. "I remember a bit of that feeling, too."

She continued, her eyes twinkling. "And then came secondary school—a whole new world. I still remember that bittersweet first day. My first class was English and Grammar, and halfway through, the teacher assigned a massive project. It felt like a nightmare! There were lockers to manage, heavy books to carry, and long lectures to sit through. But somehow, I made it through, and the relief I felt on graduation day was beyond words. When they offered me the librarian position, I jumped at it without a second thought. I'd always loved reading, and the Head Librarian was thrilled to have me as his student."

"I'm sure he was," I said, smiling. "He's been so patient with me too, and he's always encouraging. He told me just the other day that I'm a quick learner—and that I'm special. It was nice to hear."

"Yeah, he is a remarkable man," Molly agreed. "A little mysterious, maybe, but kind. Now, tell me, do you feel a bit better, Julia? I wanted to show you that every big moment comes with its challenges, but the rewards are always worth it. Does that help ease your nerves a bit?"

"It does, actually," I said, feeling a weight lift. "Thank you so much."

"It's no big deal," she replied with a wink. Then, with a mischievous glint, she added, "Now, there's one more thing you absolutely need to do."

I raised an eyebrow, curious. She met my gaze with a grin and simply said, "Go to bed, Julia."

CHAPTER 9

Jack

I stood up and yet again found myself in a tall stretch. I had been seated throughout the afternoon pouring over literature and Underground policy documentation. My back was feeling the effects from sitting so poorly for so long. Growing older mostly just made me realize how fast time slips past you. Once you realize this, it's usually too late and it's just gone. I took my glasses off and rubbed my eyes, forcing them to remain focused and alert. I had a plan on what I was going to present to the Council in a matter of hours. I was confident in my presentation, but less so in the Council itself. Part of me feels like things began to shift when the current Counselor took office. In the years prior, I have experienced a few different leaders, and they all do have their own agendas, sometimes making it hard to navigate and prioritize important aspects that need clear, concise decisions.

The most tumultuous Counselor was actually my father-in-law. In general, Counselor's choose their successors, and as they aged out, the transition period would begin. Sarah's father was a prominent figure in the Council so I was not surprised by the news of his promotion. I was not yet on the Council myself, so he viewed me as an inferior and rejected any idea I would suggest without even considering it. At the time, I was still a young man, and was rapidly gaining strength both mentally as well as physically. The Librarian training included a significant amount of physical fitness in addition to the extensive reading. With this training I became more assertive in my convictions. I held my head high and was able to hold my ground in our debates. I had continued to pour myself into literature heavy in philosophy, history, and economics, and my knowledge had grown exponentially. However, this had little to no effect on his views of me, as his son-in-law.

My father-in-law had very prudish, old-fashioned ideas and it hurled the entire community backwards in terms of innovations and citizen rights. He was traditional in terms of how he wanted family units to operate. He was not tolerant of individual thought or anything that operated outside of his mapped out agenda. This became a constant battle as my wife had always been all of the things he was now trying to discourage or outright banish. When he became Counselor it was detrimental to our family, and caused a big rift between us all.

It also happened to coincide with a time in our own marriage that was also the rockiest and the hardest to overcome. Sarah and I both really did want a child. I was initially unsure about the idea of bringing a child into this community, but Sarah was adamant. She wanted to pour her love into something that would bond us forever. Of course I could not refuse her and the hope began.

We had been trying to conceive for months. It was probably a total coincidence, but other couples around us were constantly announcing the joyous news of their pregnancies. We would plaster happy faces, giving our support, but inside we were in pain. A pain that built up walls between us as time went on. A pain that caused hurt in more ways than one. She began to resent me and place blame at my feet. I would question her loyalty and ask why I was not enough for her. We both knew we could not continue under such intense feelings of hurt that bounced between us. So we sought out help.

Help first sent us to the infirmary. They, as expected, ran numerous tests on both of us. They encouraged us to stay positive, that anything could be overcome. Pumping us full of hope and reassurances we would return home with a newfound level of excitement at again the possibilities we had dreamt for our future. The results were never clear. The infirmary was of no help.

We went to her parents and tried our best to explain the dilemma we were facing. Sarah's mother wouldn't hear of it at all. She excused herself, stating that those were private matters and shouldn't be discussed so out in the open. Sarah shrank inwardly at the admonishment she received from her mother. Her father, who had just become the Counselor, also was visibly uncomfortable at the topic at hand. He would shift his position in the chair, and try to offer words of comfort to his daughter, as best as he knew how. Sarah pleaded with him to help us. We were willing to take in a child in need. She was so used to him granting her every desire, she was devastated when for the first time her request was denied.

She fell into a deep state of depression. I couldn't reach her. She stayed in the confines of our apartment for weeks. She barely ate, barely bathed, barely got out of bed. I would bring her all of her favorites, in hopes to see just the faintest glimpse of a smile. Massive bouquets of daisies cluttered our entire apartment. I brought her favorite sweets to her bedside but they remained untouched. I was at a loss and my sadness loomed over me everywhere I went.

I searched high and low in the private library for anything that could help me help my wife. I read any book that even hinted at women's struggle, women's empowerment, women's rights. I needed something to spark a light back into her so she could see the purpose in her life again. And that's when I found it. I was sure of it. It was centuries old, the cover faded and frail but I was hopeful that this book would be the key to bringing my wife back to me.

The collective book contained an essay called "A Room of One's Own," written by Virginia Woolf. It was thought provoking. She could not help but listen and engage. She understood the philosophies that were printed on the pages and began to paint them in her mind's eye. She could relate to the struggles these women must have endured. By the end of the essay we were both in tears. I, mostly because I was never able to control my emotions in her presence. She saw my face and smiled for the first time in months. She looked into my eyes and we stayed like that for a long while. I would've been happy to stay like that forever.

Looking back, I'm relieved that the current Counselor is more progressive and liberal in many ways that the previous leaders had not been. He assumed the role at an unusually young age compared to his predecessors, each of whom were typically older and more traditional in their approach. His style is strikingly theatrical, and he keeps himself shrouded in an air of mystery. Figuratively and literally, he remains hidden away, secluded from the public eye. He's taken control of an entire wing of the executive level, crafting a private sanctuary where his every need is catered to and everything he requires is brought in, eliminating the need to leave his domain.

This reclusiveness, paired with his habit of wearing dramatic robes that obscure his face, adds to his enigmatic aura. Even his speech carries an air of authority and intimidation, a calculated move to assert dominance. This layer of mystery not only feeds the curiosity of the citizens but has won him an almost effortless respect. To the community, he is a powerful, almost untouchable figure, and this distance fosters an unquestioning trust in his leadership.

His governance style is unlike anything we've seen. Unlike previous Counselors, his focus doesn't seem to be on the day-to-day concerns or well-being of the citizens. Instead, he's passed most routine responsibilities down the line—to the Council and, ultimately, to the Committee. In his eyes, these tasks are trivial, not worthy of his direct involvement. Surprisingly, even with his minimal oversight, things continue to function smoothly, as his lack of interest has barely altered day-to-day operations.

But his policies on matters of the Above are deeply concerning to me. His continual efforts to instill fear throughout the community unsettles me. Every suggestion he makes to the Council is rooted in fear and control. His latest proposal is to implement a high-tech surveillance system throughout the Underground. He wants hidden cameras in every public space, monitoring every activity, every citizen—without their knowledge. He argues that this system could help detect threats from the Above, should an invasion ever occur, and he's insisting that I oversee this surveillance from a mainframe, reporting any "suspicious" activities to the Council. Naturally, he also wants a direct monitor installed in his private quarters, purely "for viewing purposes," as he put it.

Using the potential danger from the Above to justify this level of surveillance is manipulative and deeply troubling. Such an invasive measure not only violates every citizen's privacy, but also reveals an underlying distrust that could fracture the community if left unchecked. With each passing month, his influence grows, and he's gathering support slowly, even managing to sway some Council members to back his extreme policies. Currently, the Council is split on his proposal, but the balance is precarious, and momentum seems to be shifting in his favor.

What I find most intriguing is that, as a child, no one would have predicted he'd rise to such power. He's done his utmost to erase any traces of his younger self —no photos, no records, no stories from his school days remain. It was almost effortless for him to vanish from collective memory because, in truth, he was barely noticeable even then. He was the kid who blended into the background, an unremarkable face in a crowded room. His parents were also of modest means—his mother worked in laundry, and his father in sanitation. Neither role held any particular status within the community. It wasn't until after school that he began to exude a superiority complex and started gathering followers, captivated by his increasingly radical ideas.

It was his outcast status in his youth that seemed to give rise to this hunger for influence. What was once an invisible presence in the community became a formidable figure. Sarah's father recognized his potential early on and welcomed him into his inner circle, granting him access to resources and information he otherwise wouldn't have had. This access allowed him to rise, gathering more power with each passing year.

Just then, the evening alarm sounded, signaling to all residents that it was time to return to their apartments. For me, it meant the time had come for my meeting—a meeting that could very well have serious consequences for an unfortunate citizen.

CHAPTER 10

Jack

I gathered all of my research and stuffed it into my briefcase. I also grabbed the report I had written up that summarized the log sheets I had picked up earlier in the day. I first needed to make a quick stop to drop this report off at the Sub's office. The Sub, or Subordinate, is the second hand man to the Counselor. He is also hand picked by the Counselor and is his main point of contact, or should I say, a way to filter information through without him having to deal with anyone or anything directly. The Sub also just happens to be my closest friend, Henry.

He is 20 years my junior, but we have established our friendship over the years and have always bonded through the ups and downs we both have encountered. He usually stands with me on my views on policy, but this does tend to infuriate the Counselor. Because of this, he tries to tread lightly in public settings. The Counselor does place value in his opinions and is most open to considering an alternative idea if it comes from him. I have never pried into how their actual relationship was formed, nor how it is so interestingly maintained. Nonetheless, I am pleased to be able to have open conversations with him and have intellectual debates without either of us taking a firm stance one way versus the other, or without taking the issue at hand personally.

He has had a difficult time during his adult life and I was happy to assist him in any way I could. If nothing else but to provide emotional support and an ear to listen. I have always kept his secrets and held in the utmost confidence anything he divulges to me. I became his mentor, advocate, and protector without either of us truly realizing it. I have his back, and he has mine. He has been there for me, and was a shoulder for me to lean on when I finally did lose Sarah. The adjustment to being on my own after all those years spent together was something I had never wanted to imagine. Having a friend to lean on was the only thing that pulled me through.

Henry's office was located on the executive residence level, as it was included in the wing that the Counselor occupied. This was very much for convenience purposes and he was constantly at the Counselor's disposal. The walk from my apartment to his office was quick, leaving plenty of time for us both to get to the meeting on time. I gave a couple of taps on the door and proceeded to open and enter before hearing a reply. It was mostly a courtesy knock anyway. He looked up and smiled at my arrival and motioned for me to sit opposite him.

He was seated behind an oversized executive desk. The top was completely covered by papers strewn and piled about. He liked to call it his organized mess. It gave me anxiety. I can be as messy as the next guy, but by the end of the day I have my mess in order. At this point, I was used to his disarray and expected nothing else. He was a very nice looking middle aged man who kept himself fit, clean shaven, and nicely dressed at all times. He was the ultimate beacon of society...or of the Underground I should say. He was the model citizen and role model to anyone he might encounter. He would volunteer his time by visiting the schools, stopping by and talking with patients in the infirmary, or just by hanging out in the cafeteria or the lounge and getting to know the younger crowd who tended to use those spaces. He was quick to laugh and was so easy going it was nearly impossible to dislike him. This made him a valuable asset to the Counselor as well.

I handed Henry the report that outlined the progress the two librarians working under my mentorship had made. He pretended that they were of equal interest, but we both knew his only concern was for Julia. I always played along and spoke about both of them. The other librarian's name is Molly. It was the first time I had ever had two women working under my mentorship. She was twice Julia's age and very friendly and sincere. She has a good head on her shoulders, is easy to get along with and has the potential to be a greater leader within the community. This was shown by how easily she took Julia under her wing. They worked very well together and I can see the fondness Julia has for her. She is currently not completely dedicated to her duties, as she has a different sort of distraction. She is at the age, which is completely understandable and of no fault of her own, where her family life has taken a bigger priority. She has a young child and I am sure balancing both the care for her child and taking on the responsibilities at the library, as well as carving out time for Julia, can be a lot to juggle. I see no problem in giving her as much leeway as she needs. After all, this is why I have two librarians to pull from. No one should have to commit to such a role all of the time, especially when personal life comes into play. I have told her that as long as she stays up on her weapons training, the rest can be flexible to accommodate both of our schedules. I know this is a temporary situation, as it is usually just until the child enters school age, so I am willing to give her this with no questions asked.

As such, my report states that Molly's performance is satisfactory, whereas Julia has exceeded what was required. She has been putting in far above what is the standard for practicing and the results are showing in her overall performance. Henry was pleased with this news and wanted to hear more anecdotes about Julia. This was a common request and he always seemed fascinated with stories that illuminated features of her personality or other unique qualities she possessed.

It seems that he is intent on gathering as much information about her as possible, without having any actual desire to meet her in person, which he could easily do.

I proceeded to tell him a prepared story. During one of our training sessions a few weeks ago, Julia had arrived a little late, which was completely out of the norm for her. I assured him that she is typically respectful of my time and her punctuality is very important to her. Regardless, this one and only instance, she had run into the training room completely frazzled and out of breath. She immediately apologized over and over again and promised that it would never happen again. I found myself half listening as I could not figure out what it was that was different about her. Her hair was the same sandy brown hair, and it was styled similarly to how she normally wore it in a low ponytail. Her brown eyes darted at me, desperate for forgiveness, of which I gladly gave. If for nothing else except to ease her anxiety. The satchel she normally wore across her body was in her hand and it swayed beside her as she began pacing, deciding whether or not she should confide in me what had happened. My eyes, usually not too astute to fashion, finally saw what her dilemma was. I figured it out before she even had to tell me. It was obvious. Her white dress was a complete mess. She was clearly attempting another one of her sewing projects and it had just gone way wrong. She saw me squinting at it and embarrassingly commented that yes, she had tried attaching a button down shirt onto one of her already made skirts, therefore turning it into a dress, and that well...it didn't work out so well. The buttons were misaligned, the hem was uneven, one sleeve length was longer than the other, and the list could go on. I didn't even know how it was possible to mess up the top that horribly when the shirt itself should've remained intact. I was trying my best to not laugh at the overall state of her, but my eyes gave it away. She was the first to break into laughter and as she looked down at herself she just threw her arms up, and said well, guess I won't be modeling this look anytime soon. I was grateful to be able to laugh with her, because I was really struggling to contain it.

The story was enough to satisfactorily amuse Henry and he thanked me for sharing such an entertaining encounter. The two of us rose at that and began our walk down to the Council meeting.

CHAPTER 11

Jack

The meetings were held in the Great Hall, the same space that was shared for the big event. Walking into the hall I noticed that everything was indeed set up and the only thing that was left to do was bring out the food and drinks prior to the start. In the back corner they had arranged a special area for the purpose of our meeting. We arrived on time, but the majority of the Council was already seated and waiting for the meeting to begin. The Council was made up of twenty members, all men. The tables were arranged in the shape of a large U and the Counselor's seat was positioned in the opening of this U. The assigned seating was such that more key members sat in closer proximity to the Counselor. The Sub sat to his right, and I sat to the right of the Sub, and everyone was right of me until the U was completed round to the other side.

The Counselor made his way into the room and the meeting was underway. Anyone who wanted to was allowed a chance to speak but they were required to stand in order to address the group. The topic at hand was the Selection and the way in which candidates should be chosen. Many in the group were content with how it's always been done and didn't see the reasoning behind making any changes. The Counselor said he was bored of this "tradition" and wanted to make it more exciting. He was throwing out ideas to make it into more of a spectacle, or even into an activity in which there was a winner and a loser. The Council questioned this idea of a contest as it wasn't clear if the winner became the chosen one, or if it was the loser who was to leave the Underground. Of course, all this frustrated the Counselor. He did not like to be questioned or challenged.

As the squabbling in the room died down I rose to address the Council myself. I proposed that we still celebrate the Selection and the meaning that the Selection represented, but that we give up the idea that a citizen be chosen to face the task that the Counselor hands down to that person year after year. The room became silent as this had never even been considered and I could tell they were dumbfounded. Henry chimed in to break the silence and added that it was an interesting change and worth considering. Since no one else spoke, I continued to give examples of other societies and how we too could adapt and create new traditions and find other ways to create a peaceful coexistence with the Above. I also suggested that instead of the Council casting votes for who they want the chosen individual to be, that the chosen be from a list of volunteers. Volunteers who were willing and able to take the challenge on. I was certain there would be more than enough individuals who would jump at the opportunity. I sat back down as I let my words drift over them and let it simmer in their minds.

The Counselor finally addressed the room. He began by stating that he enjoyed listening to me speak and appreciated me sharing my findings with the group. He thanked me and said I had good ideas, ideas he could work with, ideas he could use to come up with his own ideas. The meeting then abruptly came to an end as he rose from his seat and briskly walked out of the Hall. He was gone so fast that it left the rest of us still remaining in place.

Henry and I looked at each other and I could see that he was equally concerned and confused by what had just occurred. We all filed out in silence and together walked down the one flight of stairs to the executive level and one by one went inside our own apartments. I entered my apartment and upon closing the door, I felt like I was finally able to breathe again. The Council had so much unpredictability and was so stressful that being in this group alone was aging me significantly. I was constantly wishing I was able to resign but I knew this would never be accepted. The Head Librarian is a fixture on the Council and they went hand in hand.

At that moment, I missed Sarah. It was always immediately when I arrived home to an empty apartment. I missed her scent, the freshness of soap and flowers. I missed being able to share our burdens with one another. I then realized why she journaled and what that did for her. I had always respected her privacy and had never even dared to try and read any of her entries...but something was pulling me towards her desk and the temptation to do so now was too overwhelming. So I did. Just the very last entry. It was addressed to me.

My dearest Jack,

I hope you finally got up the nerve to enter my journal and find that I have left this entry for you, and you alone. Firstly, know that my love for you will always be limitless and I have zero regrets. You fulfilled my life to the fullest and I was so lucky to have been caught by you on that very memorable Selection day.

It was the very first time we met, the very first time our eyes met, the very first time I was held in your arms. You gave me a chance to grow and learn beside you and for that I am forever grateful. You are the most special man I have ever met and a true gem within the community. Please find some peace for yourself now. Find peace in my words. Find peace in the love that filled my entire lifetime and beyond. Be happy. Find happiness. Do whatever it takes to get to the places you need to be. Don't let anyone stop you. Time is precious, and you my dearest, are the most precious of all.

Your forever shining star,
Sarah

A single tear rolled down my cheek and onto the entry, smudging the ink beneath. I would memorize these words, her instructions. I would instill them so deeply into my heart that it would give me the strength to find my way forward. I went to sleep still cherishing the gift she had left for me.

CHAPTER 12

Julia

The mirror reflected someone I recognized, but also something different. A new version of myself. This new me represented a more grown up, sophisticated, strong, and courageous person. I saw in the mirror a beautiful young woman, who knew what she was doing with her life, no longer an innocent girl who spent all of her time behind a book.

Admiring myself in the dress I had finished the previous day, I couldn't help but feel gorgeous in it. As the last finishing touch, I grabbed a special, more intricate satchel to hold my hatchet, as it was a more fitting accessory for such a special event. After I put on my satchel, I looked at myself one more time in the mirror. My mother's necklace shimmered in the light of my room. Feeling satisfied, a smile beamed across my face as I turned around and walked out of my room ready to greet my father and face the day ahead.

When he saw me, his eyes shone with happiness and pride, "You look beautiful, Julia."

"Thank you," I responded, slightly embarrassed.

"I know neither of us knew your mother," he said, "But I think if she saw you now, she would be so proud of you."

Those words meant a lot to me. I had only a few dim memories of what my mother was like, but I often wondered what life would be like if she were still alive. What kind of person would she be? What would she think of me? What would our relationship be like? Even as my father spoke, part of me felt as though the words were coming directly from her.

We walked side by side making our way down to the gateway of the Great Hall where the Selection took place. We stopped directly in front of the doors and looked at each other.

"Ready?" my father asked.

"Ready as I'll ever be," I joked, holding his hand in mine.

Together, we entered a crowded room, filled with every single resident of the Underground. The multitude of people blended together in a sea of white. The women were wearing long, elegant dresses, and the girls were dressed similarly, although with knee-length dresses. The men were wearing distinguished looking linen suits, and finally, nice pants and dress shirts for younger boys. Despite looking so similar these were people with different occupations, interests, and private lives. They all milled around long tables spread around the large hall, eating cakes and sandwiches and other delicious desserts and foods.

All eyes eventually made their way to the main attraction of the Selection, a magnificent stage set in the middle of the room. Once a year, the leader of the Underground, known as the Counselor, speaks directly to the society, and it is on this day that he chooses the one to complete a very special task. Some found being chosen an honor, while it was a nightmare for others since the task was dangerous and potentially life-threatening. Speculation has always been abundant on where or what becomes of the chosen one. All those who had been chosen in the past had left, never to return. Rumors always circulate that the chosen don't return because they have joined forces with our greatest enemies, the people who don't live under the surface. The people of the Above are an ever present threat to our society, at least that's what the Counselor and community leaders warn. Hence, the Selection process had been created. One person is chosen for the purpose of representing the Underground to maintain the brittle peace with the Above. My father, clearly with this in mind, was very smart in sharing the plan with me on how we would be able to reunite if one of us was the chosen one this year.

Upon entering, my dad was greeted by various members, while I continued to scan the room for my friends. Quite surprisingly, a voice beside me spoke, "Ms. Brown?" I turned to face the Head Librarian. He always managed to sneak up on me and startle me in the most eerie way.

As he now had my attention he continued, "Are you enjoying the event?"

"Oh, yes I am," I managed to blurt out, "It's absolutely wonderful. The maintenance crew did a great job setting up this year."

"Hmmm, yes. The maintenance crew."

He paused, giving this some thought and continued, "Your friend Leo is part of that I assume. You keep interesting company to be sure. I do hope you spend your time wisely."

Geez, where do I begin with this!?! Questions swirled in my head as he clearly was hurling judgments my way! But, rather smartly, I composed my defensive, screaming brain by changing the subject. I motioned over to my father to basically come rescue me. I asked him, "I suppose you have never met my father?"

"It's very nice to meet you, sir," my dad jumped right in, smiling, extending his hand to shake, "My name is David. David Brown. Julia has said nothing but wonderful things about the library and her time there."

"Pleasure, Mr. Brown," the Head Librarian responded, shaking my father's hand. He then glanced at me, then my necklace, and continued, "Yes, Julia has much to learn. Much to learn in not enough time. But, nonetheless, I must apologize. I must begin the security protocols and check in with some other acquaintances. Please, enjoy your night."

And with that, he briskly walked away.

"It's completely fine," my father said after him, "I hope you enjoy your night!"

While I was still processing the bizarre exchange that had just occurred, my father happily turned to me and said, "I need to go find some colleagues before the ceremony begins. Are you ok on your own for a bit?"

I nodded, and as we parted ways, I was left standing alone. I then realized that I too was supposed to be hyper focused on any potential threat during the Selection as well. Maybe that is why the Head Librarian warned me to spend my time wisely?

I adjusted my satchel and made sure my hatchet was still secure and began to weave through the crowd. I finally spotted June standing next to her father, who was happily chatting with a group of community officials. She, however, looked like she was going to die of boredom.

Approaching them I politely interrupted, "Hello, Mr. Dean, would it be ok if June joins me while we get something to eat?"

"Of course, Julia, dear," June's father said with a warm smile. To talk with any official of the Underground, you have to be formal and polite in every way humanly possible. Because I've made such a good impression in the past, he's always supported my friendship with June. His colleagues, however, began to stare in my direction with odd expressions on their faces. As we walked away

I heard whispers with my name being audible among them. Some people were ridiculous. Clearly the rumors were still circulating through the community.

The moment June and I were far enough away, June let out a huge, "Thank you so much! They were talking about the same old boring politics, as always. Anyway, you look amazing, Julia! Did you make this dress? You didn't tell me you were making a dress for the Selection this year!"

"June! You are going a mile a minute! Yes, I made the dress; thank you for the compliment," I answered as I gave her a little twirl and curtsy.

"No problem, girl!" my best friend replied with a grin on her face. The two of us hugged, and I began to look around for Leo. Instantly, I saw him in the back corner of the hall with a drink in his hand, also looking rather bored. Grabbing June's arm, I pulled her towards that direction. She kicked and pulled away in protest, but somehow I managed to hold on to her. When we reached Leo, I let go of her, and she put a grumpy expression on her face. My annoyance at her disappeared when I looked up at Leo and smiled at him. He smiled back.

"You look beautiful," he complimented me.

"Thank you," I responded, blushing slightly. Leo leaned towards me, kissing me slowly. Closing my eyes, I kissed him back softly, placing my right hand gently on his cheek while he held my hips.

"Ew," June stated, "I did not need to see that. You

two need to get a room."

"But June," I replied with a laugh, "We're in a room right now. Every single second of every single day, we are in a room. So it doesn't matter where Leo and I kiss, does it?"

June, once again, looked away with a grumpy face, admitting her defeat quietly. Leo laughed a whole-hearted laugh, and I blushed again. Stepping away from them for a minute, I grabbed a plate from the nearby banquet table and filled it with various treats and nibbles. As I turned to return to my friends, I began to observe a small argument that had risen between June and Leo after I had left.

"You're so stupid! You can't say that to her!" Leo said, laughing very hard.

"Not as stupid as your face! You don't know what you're talking about!" June insulted back, causing me to break out into laughter as I walked up alongside Leo.

"Wow guys, the insults you both come up with are getting better and better!" I gladly interjected into their banter. They quickly realized they'd been caught and self corrected back to the basics of once again purely coexisting.

All of a sudden, the bright lights that had filled the room went completely dark. Gradually, only the center stage became illuminated and the room, that only moments before had been filled with chatter, became utterly silent. As our eyes adjusted, our gaze was drawn to the center stage where the Counselor now stood. He had a black hood covering the top half of his face, but I could still see a wide smile on his face as he began the Selection.

"Good evening, wonderful ladies and gentlemen of the Underground," the crowd cheered in response to his greeting, "This year's Selection has been altered slightly to create a more dynamic opportunity, so as to make sure everyone's voices are heard. I will call the names of four individuals above the age of 18, and they will come to the stage and stand beside me. Members, you will then cheer for the individual you would like to promote for the Selection. The person who receives the loudest recognition will become the chosen one, to go on their quest to save us from the cruelty of the Above!"

While some in the crowd roared in excitement, others whispered and gossiped, but I stood in disbelief. I clung to Leo and held June's hand as she squeezed mine in reassurance. This was not a good change at all. This meant that there was a larger chance one of my friends or I was going to be chosen. We might die. We might never see the Underground again. The Counselor raised his arms up, silencing the community, and began calling names.

"The first name. Rebecca S.! Come forward!"

A quiet murmur arose as a young woman in her early 20s walked nervously onto the stage.

"Next, Daniel M.!"

While a group of men, clearly all friends, cheered him on, a man in his 30s strolled rather confidently up to take his place. Only two more to go. I could do this.

"Third is Nathan L.! Come forward!"

A boy my age walked up, and I actually recognized him. I went to school with this boy, and seeing someone walk on stage that I knew personally was a bit unnerving. I noticed that his mother was in tears and in obvious torment. The remaining family members all huddled around her trying their best to comfort her and convince her that this was an honor. All other thoughts were on the one remaining lingering question that remained. Who would be the final person called upon?

"And finally...Julia B.!"

CHAPTER 13

Jack

The mirror showed someone I recognized, but also someone who had aged, wrinkles deeply set into my face, but my eyes had somehow become clearer, and my overall physique and mental prowess had grown stronger. The mirror reflected an aging wise man, who still had a lot of life ahead him, things to accomplish, improvements to work towards, and people to protect.

I was preparing for the day ahead and whatever game was about to be played. I was completely kept in the dark regarding this year's Selection. The meeting was, as far as I can tell, a failure. Maybe it was too much to ask of them. Eliminating such a significant yearly tradition which brought the community together would cause some waves, but nothing that couldn't be overcome. Maybe over time, the idea would gradually work its way in and we could stop losing citizens for no reason. Perhaps, if one of the Councilmen lost their own child to the Selection they would be more open to consider such a change. I wouldn't give up and I would continue to advocate for the community, even if no one agreed with me.

I let out a big sigh and proceeded to head to the special occasion. The words from the letter that Sarah left me still rang in my head and I couldn't help but replay the first time we met. I was still fairly new to being a librarian, and still completely awkward and uncomfortable in social settings. All citizens are required to attend the Selection, so I was forced to be there. Everything was always the same at this event. The Hall was set up so there was plenty of food and drinks to go around, the stage was prominently featured in the middle of the Hall, and there was an excited chatter everywhere around the space. Happy laughter, children running around playing games, women in their finest of dress, men also wearing white linen suits. People would tend to congregate with others from within their own departments. Officials huddled together deep in conversation, the ladies of the tailoring department would be quietly gossiping and giggling to one another.

The Counselor would come on stage and announce who they had picked to be the chosen one and that person would come on stage and everyone would cheer and congratulate them. That person would then be ushered off the stage as everyone else in the community would continue with the celebrations. I usually was content to stay very close to the exit door just biding my time until I felt safe, firstly that I wasn't the selected individual, and secondly until I knew no one would miss my absence. On this particular Selection, there was more rowdiness to the event and the younger people were more physically engaged. There was some pushing and shoving, a momentum to get closer and closer to the stage's edge, creating a compact mob.

That's when I saw her. Sarah. She was getting swept up into this chaos created all around her. I rushed as fast as I could to reach her. Just as she was about to lose her balance, I reached out my arms and I caught her midair. I was out of breath and she was beyond startled. Not only by her actual fall, but more so that she had been safely caught. We looked into each other's eyes and I instantly knew my life would never be the same. She was the answer to my future and that thing I didn't even truly know I was missing from my life. I leaned her back onto her feet and she smiled shyly at me. I asked her if she was ok, and she nodded and tried to respond but the Hall was too loud for me to hear. I grabbed her hand and we both exited the Selection.

I led her to the elevator, telling her there was something I wanted to show her. She willingly, but nervously agreed to come with me. I took her to level -9. We entered the library and I proceeded to unlock the backroom. Her eyes widened with surprise as she had never been to this space and was unsure what to expect. I took her through, directly into the private library. Her eyes lit up like shining stars and she was overwhelmed. Her beauty in that moment, in the white beautiful gown that perfectly draped her petite frame was a memory that would be etched into my mind forever. She had a million different questions which I amusingly answered one at a time. I told her she could come back as often as she liked, of which she did. It was through this connection that the bond between us grew and grew, and it grew into a love that was beyond my wildest dreams.

I already had low expectations for this year's Selection. It almost felt like comparing it to what it must be like to attend a magic show, having no way to know what the Counselor was going to pull out of his hat. Upon entering the room there was absolutely nothing out of place, or out of the ordinary. Julia just happened to be directly in front of me as I entered the Hall. She was scanning the room and I approached her, interrupting her thoughts. We made pleasantries and, as I do question her choices in friends, I was clearly making her uncomfortable so her father joined us. He is a wonderful person, a wonderful contributor to the community, and a wonderful father. I have to admit, my father-in-law chose the correct person to raise Julia. I quickly excused myself as I really did need to move on. There is no real need for any type of security during these events. I did, however, really need to find Henry as soon as possible.

I actively avoided the group of Councilmen that were standing idly together and crossed the Hall opposite them. My eyes could not pinpoint Henry anywhere and I wondered if he had not yet arrived. I briefly considered messaging him, but the watches were an overall annoyance that I also actively avoided using. I was about to leave the Hall and head back down to see if I could catch him in his office, when I spotted him walking towards and joining the group of already congregated Councilmen. Of course, that is where he would end up. As I turned to walk in that direction, the lights went dark and the "show" was about to begin. Oh, the dramatics. He just can't help himself. Since I happened to be near my favorite spot in the Hall, near the exit door, that is where I made camp, arms crossed and with a small scowl on my face. My talk with Henry would have to wait.

The Counselor made his announcement. Community involvement to decide who is to be chosen this year. Well, I suppose it could've been worse. His other ideas were definitely more extreme so perhaps he came to this after hearing me talk? Or perhaps Henry did get to him after all. He began calling the names of the potential candidates. I am unsure how he came to pick these four individuals but I'll try and find that out later. Then it happened. My worst fear. The last name he called was Julia.

CHAPTER 14

Julia

My heart sank at the Counselor's words and I grew instantly pale. I felt the eyes of the Underground society shift to me. I separated myself from my two closest friends and began to slowly move towards the stage, forcing one foot in front of the other. I couldn't bring myself to see the look in Leo's eyes, or the expression that was surely blanketing June's face. The people in the crowd thankfully became one big blur, and yet parted as I walked through. With the final name being called, the noise level grew exponentially as I got closer and closer to the stage. I felt like I was a sheep about to be slaughtered. For a moment, I saw my father. He was the only person I could place and sought out for. His face also grew pale, and he looked as though he would fall over in disbelief at any moment. He was scared for my safety, especially if I was chosen from the four on stage. How did I ever find joy in this celebration? How is anyone?

Stepping up onto the stage, I proceeded to stand next to Nathan, who grimly glanced over at me.

"This entire situation kinda sucks, doesn't it?" He

whispered to me, "It will be worse if one of us is chosen."

"Yea," I whispered, fear filling my voice. The Counselor began to speak again, preventing me from saying anything further. What happened next all felt like it happened in a fog. Like I was standing there, but I was elsewhere at the same time. Perhaps it was a defense mechanism, a premonition of what I somehow knew was to come.

The Counselor raised his arms up once again to silence the crowd, to maintain absolute control, demanding everyone's full attention.

He spoke, "Members of the Underground! It is time. We will now make this year's Selection one to remember!"

While we 4 stood on stage watching the scene in front of us unfold, the members roared in support as the Counselor continued his speech. "Each candidate will step forward individually, and members, you are to cheer collectively for who you would like to promote as this year's Selection chosen one. Very well! Let's begin."

He motioned for the first to step forward. The young woman stepped forward, head held high, and a hint of the smallest smile graced her face. The crowd seemed unsure as to what the process was, as it remained surprisingly quiet and calm. All that was heard was a low murmur of applause but not much else. This result pleased the young woman very much and her smile grew with every passing second. The Counselor excused her and asked her to return to her position.

Next the Counselor asked the man to come forward. He actually looked more nervous now than when he first came on stage. As previously, his friends, who clearly occupied the bulk of the space most nearest to the stage, began to roar with laughter and screams. Screaming his name so much so that it actually became a chant. Luckily for the man, the chant did not catch on or grow throughout the community, and it stayed pretty isolated amongst the man's "friends." He looked rather embarrassed by the entire spectacle and became very flushed. He was also asked to step back, and was visibly relieved and thankful for the experience to end.

Nathan was next.

As Nathan stepped forward I couldn't help but glance over at the candidates beside me and think that it was such an odd mix of candidate choices. All relatively young, all with different jobs, 2 men, and 2 women. How do they even determine who is chosen? Is it a lottery system? I already knew that the answers didn't even matter, because this was happening whether I liked it or not.

Nathan approached the front of the stage and the cheers picked up more audibly. It began as a slow roll from the back of the hall, building momentum as it reached the stage. Nathan could also notice the audible difference and I was close enough to see that he began to physically tremble. His face was expressionless, and he dared not look up from the spot he stared at on the ground in front of his shoes. The Counselor at once became pleased with the growing interest and response from the members. Nathan was excused.

I knew what this meant. This means all eyes were going to be fixed back onto me. This felt like torture in so many ways. The Counselor motioned for me repeatedly to come forward and I reluctantly obeyed. As I approached the spot, the same spot the 3 previous "victims" had stood at, it became uncomfortably still and quiet. You could hear the random cough interrupt the silence that had ensued. I stood and waited to hear the response and how it would determine my future. The noise erupted simultaneously from my left and my right, and then grew as it quickly overcame the hall. Looking out into the crowd, I saw happy, excited faces. They were cheering for me. They had faces of joy and happiness. They see this chance as an award or an accomplishment. They are cheering for me because they want me to win. They want to choose me for the Selection.

The crowd quickly realized I was the chosen person, and they began to cheer even louder all together, all at once. The loud sounds of the Selection rang in my ears, my heart beating progressively faster. That was when I realized what had happened.

Oh no.

"Let's congratulate our chosen citizen..." the Counselor yelled to the audience, "Julia Brown!"

With a blank face, I looked up towards him as he stepped beside me. I stood there, a representative of the Underground, like all of the other chosen citizens had done before me. He smiled down at me, and I faked a smile back, all the while a knot growing bigger and bigger in the pit of my stomach.

"Well, what do you have to say, Julia?" the Counselor asked me.

"This entire situation is unreal," I lied, "It feels amazing to have the chance to help my society in such a big way. It is an honor. Thank you, Counselor."

"Please proceed through the doors at the end of the stage and you will be given your instructions," he directed me, that haunting smile, fixated on his face. I nodded, then turned around very robotically. I had never paid any attention in previous years that there was a door to the rear of the stage where the chosen were to exit. In years past, I remembered just hanging with lots of friends from school, and eating, joking, and enjoying the experience as it was the biggest event of the year.

Walking through those doors now though, I left behind the cheering, celebratory noises of the community I cherished so dearly, and instead started a countdown of the days I had left before I undoubtedly died.

I would cherish those moments.

Closing the door behind me, I turned to come face to face with the Head Librarian. Today was just too much.

I was numb to what had just happened, and although it was nice to see his face, he also looked overly concerned and for the first time since I've known him, completely frazzled. There was a sense of urgency to everything about him.

"Julia, are you ok?" he quickly asked. I nodded as finding my voice had been a struggle ever since my name had been called just minutes before. He continued, "Ok, good. Come with me? I have a plan. I will find a way to ensure your safe passage out of the Underground and to the Above."

"What? How?" and Why?" was all I could think to utter. So many questions came flowing out of me and I couldn't get them out quick enough.

"Julia, there's no time. You have to trust me now. Do you trust me?" he questioned. Again I nodded, but slower as I was very apprehensive. He was about to grab my hand when a figure appeared next to us, seemingly out of nowhere.

This would make things difficult.

CHAPTER 15

Jack

Watching her make her way to the stage was gut wrenching. My heart couldn't take anymore pain, or loss for that matter. Seeing her stand in a line up of four, she looked so young and innocent, so out of place. All four were too young for that matter, and definitely undeserving of the attention and pressure they were facing. There is absolutely no way any one of them was old enough to face the journey they were to be sent out on, nor have the diplomatic skills required to negotiate any resemblance of peace with the Above. It was a total farce.

I couldn't do it. I couldn't just stand there and watch Julia face what was about to happen. I instantly flashed back to the months leading up to Sarah's death and the cruelty life forces you to overcome. Initially, there had not been any significant amount of concern. She had fainted in the middle of the day. She came out of it relatively quickly but she was so weak that I had to support her to walk. I was worried about her so we went to the infirmary for the first time since we had had trouble conceiving. Thankfully, we were both always well enough that there was never a need to ask for their services. We were both on the older side by now so I guess it was only a matter of time.

Upon entering, they escorted us into a private doctor's office which was frigidly cold and sterile. The only thing in the room was a gurney, a stool, 2 metal chairs, and a metal cabinet with glass fronted doors, full of medical supplies. The Doctor entered and immediately began to ask her what her symptoms were and if she had noticed anything else unusual in her health recently. She just mentioned feeling more tired lately, but had attributed that to our ever increasing age. She had also remembered the week prior having a slight cold and a fever that lasted about a day. She assumed it was a typical virus. After hearing this he gave her a list of five objects that he wanted her to repeat, memorize, and be able to say them again whenever he asked. He looked into her eyes, listened to her breathing, and took her temperature. He was then ready for the list and she was only able to remember 2 of the 5 items.

The Doctor informed us that he was suspicious that she may be suffering from a relatively newer condition called Solar Disease, or SD. It is a condition that only affects a small minority and it is caused by a lack of UV rays from the sun. I had never even considered that living in the Underground could cause negative health effects. The doctor explained that most people who begin having symptoms find them to be short lived and they go away on their own. Only a handful became more serious conditions, and sadly they did die from the disease. The doctor gave her a small bottle of pills that she was to take daily until the course came to an end and to get plenty of rest. He was confident that she would make a full recovery.

But she didn't. Month after month we would return to the infirmary but to no avail. Just keep taking the medicine was what we were told. The medicine wasn't helping and her condition only worsened. She became even weaker and her mind began slipping in and out. One moment she would act aggressively, completely out of character, and the next she would have severe memory loss. The disease was manifesting within her body and it was winning. She knew she was dying and there was nothing I could do about it. She had good days and bad, and on the good days she tried to stay positive and in light spirits. I cherished the good days.

I went and spoke privately with the doctor. He informed me that more often than not, if the symptoms don't clear up from the medication after a month of treatment, that the patient will most likely not survive. She was dying from the darkness. Solar Disease took my wife away from me because her body needed the natural light from the sun. Not only did her mind want to be free from the Underground, but also her body, and it was giving up being constrained to this life. My heart shattered into a million pieces at the revelation. This is what took her life, and she took a part of me with her.

I couldn't stand by and feel so utterly helpless again. It felt like it was a lineup for an execution from the Dark Ages. I was one of the onlookers waiting to see what was to happen next.

A thought came to me. Maybe I was looking at this the wrong way! A revelation hit me as I stood in the back of the Hall, in front of the exit door, watching the scene in front of me. This could be her way out! This could be her chance to leave the Underground and live the life Sarah never was able to. I would help her. I wasn't sure how, yet, but I would help her somehow.

One by one, the candidates took turns receiving their support from the community. Julia was last and, based on the noise level of the previous three, I knew it was going to be her. The people were holding out for her. And I was right. I couldn't even see Julia at this point because there was so much excitement that exploded across the Hall. I weaved as quickly as I could to the side door that would be the fastest route to catch her once the madness on the stage came to an end. I had to catch her.

I had done it. I was the only person in the hallway that led out onto the stage. Within minutes she opened the door and we came face to face. Hers was a face of shock and tragedy. I wanted to fold her young frame into a tiny square and put her in my pocket for safe keeping. Anything to sneak her out of here and this horrible situation. I asked her to come with me, to trust me, and as we were about to leave, the tiny little window of opportunity shut, as another door opened and the darkly dressed figure made that impossible.

CHAPTER 16

Julia

The Counselor entered through the door and approached us. He addressed the Head Librarian directly, "Why hello there, how nice of you to check in with our newest chosen one! Looks like you will need to begin the recruiting process for the library once again. I am so sorry that this is going to cause more work for you."

The Head Librarian looked from me to him and completely naturally, smiled and responded, "Yes, I came to wish Julia good luck in person and to thank her for all of her hard work and dedication in the library. The community chose the strongest candidate this year!"

Smiling at this news, the Counselor was most pleased. The two exchanged a quick goodbye as the Head Librarian walked down a side hallway, away from me. He turned back halfway and our eyes met. I knew there was more that he needed to say. I was stuck in this moment and my loyalty was to the Selection and I had been chosen. Time to come to terms with this reality.

"Please follow me, Ms. Brown," the Counselor instructed before he began to walk down the hall. I had to half jog to keep up with his quick pace.

Suddenly, in front of one nondescript door, he stopped walking and turned, pulled out a single key, and unlocked it.

"Ladies first," the Counselor said, moving aside so I could step into the room. Inside, the walls were white and bare, and in the middle of the room was a desk. The Counselor's desk. In front of the desk sat two chairs. I sat down in one of them, while the Counselor, with a smile, sat down opposite me.

"Let us get started then, shall we?" he asked. I nodded slowly, "Well then, as you should know by now, I'm sending you to make peace with the Above. We expect you, as a member of the Underground, to uphold this community's values and represent us wholeheartedly. This is what you have been molded into throughout your time with us."

I nodded again, "Yes, I know."

"Since you are a librarian, which is a very sacred and important position to the Underground, I am allowing you the advantage of taking some additional resources, not offered to others," he said calmly, "Naturally, you should take your weapons. Additionally, to ensure you have adequate support in your vital task, I will allow you to bring along two companions of your choice. You are all to leave tomorrow."

"Really!" I cried out, both surprised and very conflicted by this news. One for the revelation that I wouldn't have to go alone, but also in a total state of panic knowing that I had to depart the very next day. I managed to muster, "Thank you, Counselor."

"It is no problem," the Counselor continued unaffected, "Now, unless there is something else, go back to your apartment and make preparations. Inform the two citizens of our decision. Farewell, Ms. Brown."

I lowered my head in respect, considering my options. The reality of the situation had not yet set in so I didn't realize the true magnitude of what was being placed on my shoulders. The Counselor was waiting so I uncomfortably stood up and walked towards the door.

"Oh, one last thing. To enter the tunnels, go to the elevator and push the -2 and -9 together simultaneously," he added, stopping me still in my tracks. Processing this information, I pondered "tunnels." What does that mean? I managed to thank him again and closed the door behind me, leaving the Counselor seated in the now completely blank space.

The hallway to leave was long. I had never known there were so many additional spaces in the Underground, especially located behind the Selection stage. I tried opening several doors along the way but with no success. They all looked identical, and they were all locked. I reached the end of the hall and in the corner most door I turned the knob just hoping this would be my way out of here. It ended up being a private stairway I had also never seen before. It was barely lit, just enough to manage, and much narrower as only one person could easily pass at a time. I peered down over the railing and it looked as though it really did access every level within the community. I decided to proceed up a couple of levels, hoping it would lead to my residential floor. Surely enough, upon leaving this mysterious stairway, the door opened into a little broom closet full of cleaning supplies. After discovering another door on the opposite side, I opened this door into the hallway that was rows of apartments. The weird thing? I was actually in the same wing of my apartment. Strangely, I had never noticed a broom closet in this section of hallway before. Looking back at the door I wondered if Leo knew about this mysterious closet and the fact that another door beyond it accessed this hidden stairway.

Trying my best to compartmentalize the situation I was currently leaving, I instead switched my focus more on what I was about to face. I entered my apartment rather bewildered and found that my dad was also struggling with the news. He was pacing back and forth and upon seeing me he pulled me into a protective embrace.

"I'm so sorry this happened, Julia," he cried, "This shouldn't be happening to you."

"Hey, it'll be okay," I comforted him, "The Counselor said I could bring my weapons with me. More importantly, I can bring two people of my choosing with me to the Above. I was thinking you could join me!"

"Jules, I can't believe that you are the one who has to face this unknown journey! I am so scared for you but I am thankful for the extra consideration and aid offered to help you along the way," my father continued looking downcast, "but sadly I cannot be one to join you."

"What do you mean?" I frantically questioned.

"I don't think I am the one who should join you," he sadly repeated, catching me completely off guard. He tried offering comfort instead, "How about you take those two friends of yours? You can still mark a path so I can follow you afterward."

"Why not you now, though?" I asked with worry.

"You'll eventually understand, Jules," he said with a small reassuring smile, "I can't explain now, but very soon, you will understand. I promise." I sat there next to him yet again feeling very deflated and overwhelmed. Full of optimism he offered, "Why don't you start packing? After that, you can get some rest. Tomorrow will be a big day for you."

How did he know I was leaving tomorrow? I never told him that. I somehow managed to arrive at my bedroom and closed the door softly behind me. I began to accumulate supplies including my favorite hatchet and a couple daggers, placing them securely in my everyday satchel. Gradually, a suspicion began to creep into my mind that there was something very important that I didn't know. It drove me crazy. In the silence of my room, I noticed that my watch was going off nonstop. Looking down and scrolling through the messages, I realized most were of course from Leo and June, a few were from Molly, and one was from a contact I didn't recognize. On this one particular anonymous message I froze, and began to question everything.

The message read: *"You are not who you think you are. You do not belong in the Underground. Escape when you get the chance, or else!"*

Reading and rereading this message over and over, the hair on the back of my neck stood up. Who could it be from and how could they assume they know more than me about my own life? I curled into a ball on my bed and tears began to flow down my face. Everything that the day had brought was too much for me to handle. I realized, with all the commotion, excitement, adrenaline, I was exhausted and found myself drifting off into a restless slumber.

A slumber which led to an even more restless dream, where more questions were raised, with no answers in sight. A dream in which I'm in my mother's arms. I can feel the security of this protective embrace and looking up, I see the glow in her piercing eyes looking directly into mine and the love that flowed between us both. We are seated somewhere dark, and everywhere around our aurora is complete darkness. The only light flickers directly above us and it is also providing a warmth to the chilly, damp air. My arms around her neck, I see the ruby necklace and it also shimmers and reflects onto the dark walls, both of us casting shadows. I am scared. She tries her best to keep me quiet. I hear yelling in the distance. An echo of a name reaches us, and it becomes louder and louder as it gets ever closer. My mother sets me down and instructs me to stay perfectly still and to not move from this spot, no matter what. I cry out in protest, but she insists and I listen obediently. She takes a lantern down from the wall and begins to walk quietly away in the opposite direction of the voices that creep towards us. She rounds the corner and vanishes along with the glow of the light that had once outlined her figure so clearly. I remained curled in a tight ball, hugging my knees...

And this is how I found myself once I had awoken. Awake to find myself in my bedroom, on my single bed. My dad must have come in to check on me at some point in the night because a blanket was softly draped on top of my curled frame. Even with this blanket I still felt cold, but I woke up to find myself in a sweat and out of breath, and the ruby necklace around my neck felt heavier somehow. I held it in my hand, searching for answers and comfort. I sat up replaying the dream in my mind. My mother was also scared. She left me alone. Why was she scared? What was she hiding from? Where did she go? What happened to her? What was the name that I heard echo throughout my entire being? A weight came over me, as did a strength that billowed over the surface. I then realized that to find out these answers I must do whatever it took in search for the truth.

Picking up my watch, I saw that I had left my friends completely hanging, and although it was early, it was imperative I talk to them immediately. I messaged them to meet me in our spot asap. Thankfully, they were also wide awake, still worried, and agreed to head straight there.

I opened my wardrobe and assessed my options. Searching to choose the final outfit I would wear to venture out of the Underground, and begin my quest to the Above. The first outfit I saw was one I had made. It was a white, button-down shirt and attached to it were a pair of white shorts, making a jumpsuit. It looked pretty baggy and square-shaped on me, but when I put on my satchel, it looked better. The outfit was also good for fighting, running, and other physical activities. It was perfect for an imperfect situation.

As I dressed, I mulled over the decision to ask my friends to put their own lives at risk. At the same time I couldn't help but ask myself...

"Why do I have to be so unlucky?"

CHAPTER 17

Jack

The Counselor interrupted and prevented my plan from taking flight. I had to switch gears so quickly and think on my feet. Luckily, my speaking with Julia made perfect sense since she does work in the library as my protege. I was forced to walk away from her though.

I went immediately back to my apartment. I could still hear the noises from the celebration continuing on in the Great Hall. The hallways were sparse because of this and for that I was thankful. I made it home, but became more and more agitated with every passing second as I began to visualize what Julia was saying, doing, feeling at this very moment. I tried to calm myself down and found myself pacing back and forth across the living room rug. I began brainstorming ideas.

The most obvious was to wait for Julia at her own apartment. She would have to go home at some point this evening. The Counselor wouldn't have her depart until probably tomorrow. I'm sure her father is worried sick as well and is waiting for her arrival. He would let me in and we could wait for her together. I could speak to both of them and convince them that she should go into hiding. Hide at my apartment until I could find her safe passage out of the Underground and to the Above.

Would her father go for that idea? I started to doubt myself and my belief that others could see beyond what the Underground offered them. Would he, or Julia for that matter, understand the risks? Or would they both see this Selection and her sacrifice as their only path forward. I was becoming more and more unsure, and I needed to be certain. I needed to have a solid, clear plan, and quickly.

I was racking my brain for any and all realistic ideas but I kept coming up blank. The only one I came up with that was even remotely feasible was that I could escort her and help her along the way. Even though this idea raised many worrisome questions, I tried convincing myself that it was practical.

I heard a quick succession of knocks on my door, interrupting all undeveloped ideas. I opened it to see Henry, who rushed inside at the sight of the smallest crack of the opening. He was beyond stressed, frantically insisting that the door be closed behind him immediately. I of course obliged, and before I could even say a word he began to desperately ask for my help. I was really trying my best to listen to him but was only picking up on specific words; Julia, the Above, tunnels, help, protect.

I forced him to sit and to take a breath and then start

again. He was visibly annoyed at me for making him pause but did as he was asked. He began again. He wanted me to leave the Underground. To find Julia, and to keep her safe. He wanted me to be her protector.

I told him of course I wanted to help Julia anyway I could but I had no idea how best to accomplish that. He replied that he had it all planned out. He reached into the breast pocket of his suit jacket and handed me a folded piece of paper. Upon unfolding it I saw a hand drawn map that had symbols to mark specific hazards and a line outlining the exact route I needed to take. He said that if I was going to do this, I had to stick to the path marked on the map, and not veer off no matter what I came across along the way. He warned that if I didn't stick to this, I would not make it out alive. As I studied the map and the intricacies of the details drawn he pulled out another curious object from the pocket of his pants. He reached forward and handed it to me. It was a metal badge with what looked like an emblem and a logo atop the rounded edge. I had never seen such a badge, emblem, or logo. He told me, if I made it, and successfully arrived to the Above, that I should present this badge to them upon entering, and I would be instantly safe and secure. He reminded me that if I agreed to do this for him, I would never be able to return to the Underground. My life would never be the same again.

I sat shell shocked. I didn't know where to begin. The first thing I wondered was how Henry knew all of this; the map, the badge, the entry point, safe entry? He could tell I was struggling, and still with an intense sense of urgency, he pushed me to make a decision. He really needed this to happen before anyone started to leave the Selection celebration. He said that if this was going to happen, I needed to pack whatever I wanted to take from this life, and about a week's worth of supplies, just to be on the safe side. He reminded me to pack light because I was going to need to carry this pack and the weight through occasionally difficult terrain.

My brain rattled with all of the information that had come at me at once. I began to rise and I looked down at the white linen suit I was wearing, and I knew I had to do this. I had to take this chance that had just been handed to me and make my way out of the Underground. I had to track down Julia and make sure that she would reach the other side as well. I'm not sure why Henry was asking this of me, but I trusted my friend and knew that there must be a reason for him to risk so much. I told him I'd do it.

I went and grabbed my pack and started to fill it with food, supplies, water and gear. I changed out of my suit into plain pants and a t-shirt, covering it all with a hooded jacket. Henry sat anxiously waiting, his leg nervously twitching. I looked around my apartment one last time, knowing it was probably the last time I would be in this space. This space where I had spent my entire adult life with the love of my life. I picked up the last journal that was left for me and I placed this carefully in the front of my pack. I went into our bedroom and walked over to my wife's dressing table. I picked up the white strand of pearls that she would wear daily around her neck. I gathered this necklace and I placed it in the same pouch as the journal. This is all I'll need. Everything else will come to me again.

Henry looked so relieved that I was ready to head out. He wanted to make a quick stop. As discreetly as possible we walked the hallway to the elevator. We took it to level -9 and he led me to the door of the armory. He unlocked the door and instructed me to grab a gun, just in case. I know I must have had a look of surprise and concern but he didn't budge. I retrieved a weapon and we then proceeded to the library. The backroom of the library to be exact. I stopped at the training facility and also put a couple of hand knives and a pocketknife in my pack. Henry, pleased with the new additions, also handed me a lantern that was sitting on the nearby counter. He then continued to lead me through the private library to the back corner of the room.

He pulled out a hidden pole of sorts that was tucked into the corner bracket of the bookcase. Raising the pole towards the ceiling, he caught the latch of the air duct vent and began to pull, opening the cover and showcasing a very wide access point. He used this same pole to catch another piece that lowered a skinny metal ladder that extended into the duct. Once these tasks were completed he turned to face me.

He embraced me wholeheartedly and said he would never be able to repay me for trusting him and agreeing to take this burden on for him. He promised that we would see each other again and that he would explain everything. Hearing that he would be a part of my future at some point brought an ounce of relief and comfort to me. He confirmed that I had the map and badge in safe keeping before ushering me to the first step of the ladder. I grasped both sides of the ladder and took a step up. He instructed me to continue up the ladder until it ran out of steps, reaching the very top. I would be passing through every level and to try to accomplish this climb as quickly and quietly as possible.

I looked up and took a deep breath and began to climb. I entered into the dark, cold hole and could hear the cover of the air duct being securely fastened below me. So this was going to be my rise to the Above.

CHAPTER 18

Julia

"What!" June yelled at me, "That's crazy! I'm flabbergasted!"

"Adding that one to a list of words to never, ever use," Leo added plainly, "What does 'flabbergasted' even mean?"

"I don't know, but it sounds cool," June says enthusiastically. Leo rolled his eyes.

"So you're saying that if we want to, we can join you on your quest to the Above," Leo said to me.

"Yeah, pretty much," I answered, feeling slightly amused that they could still manage to pick on each other in the most serious of times.

Leo responded immediately, "I was planning on sneaking off with you regardless, so obviously I'm going with you."

"Well, that was a quick answer," June commented, rolling her eyes, "If he's going, there's absolutely no way you're leaving without me too!"

"I am so relieved! You have no idea what the past 12 hours have been like for me. We have to leave today, so gather your essentials, and meet me in the library in two hours," I instructed them rather quickly, with a sense of urgency in my voice.

June immediately dashed off to pack, leaving Leo to turn and face me, "Did you make that outfit as well?"

Blush covered my face. I was wearing the jumpsuit I had made with my everyday satchel, which was holding my hatchet and daggers. He noticed what I was wearing! I'm so lucky to have such a thoughtful boyfriend.

I nodded as an answer to his question, following his question with, "Are you sure you want to come? We might never see the Underground again."

"There's no way anyone could stop me from joining you," he reassured me, "I can't imagine being apart from you so no matter what, I will stay at your side."

"I…that's so nice of you," I replied.

"Trust me, it's the bare minimum," he added, again reassuring me. I've always been so fond of his helpful nature. It is actually what attracted me in the first place. It was the end of my last year of secondary school and I was cramming for final exams, running super late to class, sprinting up the stairs of the Grand Staircase just trying to make it in one piece. When, well, the pieces fell apart. I tripped midstep, and the stack of papers and books went flying down behind me. Luckily, or unluckily, because I was so late, the stairway approaching the school level was mostly empty by that point. I began to try to scoop up all of my belongings as quickly as possible. A hand reached out holding a sizable amount of my assignments, waiting for me to collect them. I looked up and it was Leo. I knew he had already graduated the year before, and I'd seen him randomly around the community, but we never really had the same friend group to make meeting possible. I took the papers from him and thanked him, albeit shyly, barely looking at his face. I remember his smile and his kind eyes. He asked if I was ok and tried his best to relate to my situation as he recalled how stressful exam week could be. I managed to smile and thank him again and excused myself because I really was so late and had to go.

A couple of days later, we happened to run into each other in the cafeteria, and this time I wasn't a complete, chaotic mess. He smiled at me in recognition and approached me to ask how the rest of my exams had gone. I thought he was so thoughtful and sweet to ask. When he asked me if I would be up for hanging out later that evening, I obviously agreed. We've been dating ever since, and my fondness for him has only grown. And now he's willing to risk his life to accompany me on my forced excursion out of the Underground. It was the most meaningful gesture and meant the world to me.

I knew we needed to figure out packing, so I began to ramble off a mental list for both he and I, "Ok, you should go pack as well. We need food, water, any supplies we can safely bring with us. Also, change into clothes you can easily move in, just in case."

"Alright then. You know, you can be kinda bossy when you're put under pressure. I kinda like it," Leo said, winking as we walked towards the staircase.

I sighed while simultaneously fighting off the smile that he was always able to win out of me. I continued on to my apartment to pack for myself. I grabbed as many dried food bags as I could fit in my pack. I filled a case of water bottles and tied them also to the already bulging pack. As I was just finishing up, I turned around to see my father standing there, patiently watching me, holding the spool of white ribbon I had used to make my Selection dress.

"Hey Jules," he softly called, "I was thinking that this ribbon could be our marker for finding each other. Tie off pieces of ribbon along the path's wall and I will follow you, all the way to the Above."

"Woah," I gasped at it as he handed the ribbon to me, "This will work perfectly, Dad! Thank you so much!"

My father just sadly smiled, obviously hurting to see me leave. After I tied the spool to the strap of my pack, I pulled him into a tight hug.

"I'll miss you," I whispered.

"I'll miss you too, Jules," my father whispered back, "I'll see you very soon."

Upon walking out of the only home I ever knew, the hallways were still empty and quiet. I was grateful to be navigating my way down to the library without any encounters along the way. That's the last thing I needed. I was already an emotional wreck and completely stressed out. My life changed literally overnight and I don't even know what to expect in my future. I was almost to the Grand Staircase when I heard my name.

"Julia!", my dad yelled. Of course it was much louder than it needed to be, because again, we were completely alone. I turned back to see him running towards me.

"Julia," he said again, grateful to catch up to me. "Julia, I changed my mind. I don't think you should be the one to go. I will go in your place. I will go to the Above and you can stay here, where I know you'll be safe."

Looking into my dad's eyes, I could see the concern, worry, and love that was pouring out of him. His heart was breaking at the idea of losing me, and I couldn't help but to feel the same. I reminded myself that I needed to be strong, that it had to be me.

"Oh Dad, I love you too much to let you be the one to go! You know it has to be me. The community chose me. The Counselor chose me. Even if you took my place, and I stayed, how would that work? Everyone would shun me, and you would be considered a traitor as well. We would be breaking every policy regarding the Selection. It has to be me. Trust me and trust that we will find each other once this is over."

He gave me one last, long embrace, and watched me continue walking down the stairs without saying another word.

I couldn't tell my dad this, but there was another reason why it had to me. I have to get to the bottom of all of the secrets that have begun compounding over the last few days. That mysterious anonymous text was the final motivation I needed to jumpstart me into mustering up the amount of courage I know I'm going to need to get through this next phase.

I will survive, no matter what.

PART 2

Julia

CHAPTER 19

I was the first to arrive at the library, which was probably a good thing because I really needed to steady my nerves. As I began to pace, waiting for my friends to show up, I looked up just as Molly entered from the back room. She smiled when she saw me and a sense of relief exuded from her body.

"You didn't think you were going to go anywhere without saying bye to me first, were you?" she teased as she approached, her arms extended getting ready to give me a big hug.

"Molly! You have no idea! I am so so so happy to see you here! The last 24 hours have been so stressful. I don't know how I'm going to do it," I honestly confessed to her, as I embraced her gently.

"Julia, if anyone can do it, it's you. Take what you have learned here, your training, the readings, your strength. Take all of that with you. Take my belief, and your dad's belief, and your friend's beliefs. Bottle all of that up and let it empower you to never give up and reach the shimmering stars that light the skies both day and night," she lectured as tears began to stream down my cheek.

Carefully wiping them away, she continued, "You know I'm no good at goodbyes, so I'm going to just say, see you around. OK?"

I sniffled, trying my best to contain my emotions, and replied, "Yes, always."

She leaned forward kissing my forehead and swiftly walked out of the library, leaving me to stand alone yet again.

Glancing over at my abandoned pack that I had dumped near the door, I wondered to myself if I packed enough supplies. I didn't even know how long it would take to get to the Above, or any details on what the journey entailed. I was kicking myself for not asking the Counselor any questions during his super brief "info" dump. It was more like, "Congratulations, you're the chosen one. Now get out!" The fact that no one really knows anything beyond the actual Selection ceremony itself is also so odd. The ceremony's focus has always been about celebrating the chosen one and celebrating the existence of the Underground. I never stopped to think about where the chosen actually went, or why they never returned. Maybe once you leave, you're not actually welcomed back? We've never had any outsiders come into our community, again, that I know of. So maybe, because they left, they can't come back because they've been tarnished in some way. The more I thought about it, the more questions came to mind and the more fear I had as all of my unknowns remained unknowns.

Thankfully, June and Leo arrived to interrupt these thoughts, and we got straight to the task of assessing our next steps. I led them into the back room and they were awestruck. They had no idea the extent of the training facility that had been available for me and the other librarians to use. This room was exactly where we needed to be at this moment in time.

"Ok guys," I continued, "I think we should take some weapons as well. I have my tools with me already, but you both should be prepared too, just in case."

"Wow, this is so cool Julia," June exclaimed smiling, "I know I should be scared for my life right now, but I'm really excited!" As she continued assessing the space in front of her she added, "So this is where you disappear for all hours of the day. Well, I don't know about Leo, but I'm not really comfortable handling any type of weapon."

"I'm up for it! I think it'll be cool to swing some of this stuff around," Leo replied as he walked over and started experimenting with different weapons.

"Hey, this room is clearly for self-defense," my best friend pointed at while watching him, "Not for playing with them like they're toys."

"Of course," Leo said, "Now let's see. Which one should I take with me…"

"Oh goodness," June threw her arms up and basically gave up addressing him completely.

"Idiots," I muttered under my breath before

second guessing my decision and losing confidence in them both. Leo managed to regain a bit of trust by providing each of us with lanterns.

"Now these are smart and a good call," I smiled at Leo, thanking him for yet again being so thoughtful.

"Ok, while Leo's trying to decide on his weapon of choice, how about we take some additional hand knives as well?" I asked.

June optimistically replied, "I think that sounds perfect. Since those are small too it won't even weigh us down!"

I hadn't even thought about that but she was totally right. Traveling light would be hugely advantageous. After we assessed all of our packs, we felt pretty good in terms of what we had between us. We looked at each other, and I announced, "It's time to go."

They followed behind me out the library doors, down the hallway, and stood in silence as we waited for the elevator doors to open. The ding announcing its arrival broke that silence, and I realized I had been holding my breath. We walked in, and I turned, reaching out to push -9 and -2 simultaneously as the doors closed in front of us. That was probably the last time I would ever see that white hallway, full of doors, that led to the library, my favorite room in the entire Underground.

Behind me Leo and June looked at each other in nervous surprise. They also had no idea another level existed, not less by elevator. As we were lowered slowly down, the air became crisper, and the only noise now was the creek of cables swaying within the elevator shaft. The doors opened, and we looked on to see what our futures held.

The sight in front of me was absolutely terrifying. How could I do this? How could I survive? In front of me was a break in the wall of the Underground, where the perfect white walls had been replaced by a dark tunnel of stone. I couldn't see three feet in front of me. Summoning up all the courage I had, I stepped out of the elevator, my two friends joining me on either side. The elevator doors closed behind us, and I noticed that there was no call button on this level. We were stuck, and forced to move forward, into the dark unknown. Into the tunnels.

Leo thankfully broke this horrible, intense dread that was building, probably in all three of us by saying, "Well, looks like it's time to whip out the lanterns!"

As we turned them on, we began to slowly enter the mouth of the tunnel.

We walked like this for what felt like hours. Every turn looked just like the others. It was complete darkness in front and behind us. The only source of light was from the lanterns we all held in front of us, outlining the ground as we took careful steps forwards. Our surroundings were a never ending, monotonous dark gray stone. Every vantage point had a similarly sized tunnel. It was as if a gigantic animal had burrowed through the rock to create these pathways.

Although the route forward was terrifying and nerve wracking, it was also rather boring. The only interesting thing that I noticed early on were occasional markings painted onto the surface of the rock wall. None of them really made sense to any of us. They consisted of variously shaped symbols. I tried to think of anything I had come across from the books I had read, and the closest thing that I could compare them to was that of Egyptian hieroglyphics. Maybe it was from previous chosen citizens who had used them to keep track of their route too! Similarly to how I am using the ribbon given to me by my dad. I had been attaching the ribbon at random intervals along the way, but since it didn't really veer off, it was just a precaution. While walking through, it really did feel like we were in the middle of a maze, but not making any actual progress. It was tiring, and when one of us needed to stop, we'd take a break and rest for a little bit before moving on. June tended to complain the most frequently and slowed us down, but I honestly didn't mind taking my time through this…as I was afraid of whatever might be next. Surely it wasn't going to just be this easy the whole way there?

Anxieties continued to build up within all of us, and because of this Leo and June also began to argue more than I would've liked. I tried my best to ignore them as long as I could, as most times the argument would break out over the most minor issue. Ignoring them only worked for so long before it turned into too big of an annoyance. Such as this time.

June had thought she saw something in the tunnels, so she jumped up, and clung onto me, all while screaming.

"You are so pathetic, June," Leo taunted her, starting an argument.

After a minute, I got a headache and yelled, "Can both of you shut up? You're arguing over the most idiotic things ever! Why can't you two just get along!"

They were both quiet for a long time after that. So quiet that I couldn't help but get into my own head. They were clearly afraid that if they spoke another argument would ensue. In the quiet I also started to notice some oddities and wasn't sure if my eyes were playing tricks on me. Maybe there was something hiding in the shadows. I began to feel bad for yelling at them, but generally silence was better than listening to bickering.

"June, I think you might be right. I think I saw something too," I slowly spoke as I walked closer to the wall, examining it under the light. I heard it before I saw it. It was a quiet clicking or scratching sound. The longer I stood there the louder the sound became. "Guys, do you hear that? It's like something is coming closer."

Both of my friends came beside me and listened. "Yes, it's so strange," they commented almost in unison.

Then it happened. It began on the ground and then spread along the wall in front of us. It was a massive swarm of beetles. I instantly froze in place. June began backing away frantically, which I completely understood. Leo stayed by my side. The swarm collected into what looked like a river of flowing, black tar, covering every surface in its wake.

"Uh, Julia? What do we do?" asked Leo in a very uneasy tone of voice.

"June! You have to stand completely still!" I yelled after her.

The aggregation had branched off and followed after her. They began crawling up her body as she screamed hysterically. I repeated myself, "June, you have to remain calm and they will move on! Stop moving!"

"I don't know if I can!" she frighteningly responded. I walked slowly over to her side and brushed some of the insects off of her.

"Ok, now look at me and do not move," I firmly instructed. Within minutes the swarm broke away and continued down the path. My heart finally began to beat normally again. June looked absolutely traumatized so I was glad to still be standing beside her.

"Leo, are you ok? It's over now," I yelled over to him.

"Yeah, I think so. That was insane," he responded as he began to examine all of his clothes, making sure there weren't any stragglers. June however, wasn't as lucky. Large welts began to form on her skin, irritated from where the insect had obviously bitten her. She looked as if she would cry at any moment.

"I don't know if I can do this! I shouldn't be here!

Ouch, it hurts so much!" she complained while rubbing the ever growing red irritated bumps that began to visibly show.

"Oh June, I am so sorry. Try not to rub them, it will make it worse," I said as sympathetically as possible. I knew there was something I needed to apply to her skin as soon as possible, to try and ease her discomfort. We didn't even think to grab any medical supplies from the infirmary. I needed some sort of paste, so dumped the contents of my pack onto the ground. I finally saw it. I wasn't sure if it would actually help her, but it was worth a try.

"Ok June, we're going to first wash off the impacted areas. Then I'm going to use this breakfast pack and try to make a paste to put over it. Hopefully it will soothe it so it won't be as irritating," I explained.

"What is it?" she asked, still looking unsure of my idea.

"It's just oats," I answered as I continued first to wash her arms and legs, and then to mix the oats with just a little bit of water.

"Hey Leo, do you mind holding the lantern closer to her for me so I can see where to apply this?" I asked him. He gladly obliged and she stood very still for me so I could finish up.

"There, all done," I happily stated as I looked up to still see her frightened, unconvinced face. "Well, hopefully we don't have to run into, ummm, those things, again," I tried my best to reassure her.

We all thought it best to stop for the "day" and start new in the "morning", or whenever it felt like a new day as the concept of time for us was nonexistent. We lost complete track of time, as our watches had stopped working as soon as we entered the tunnels. We would just rest when we felt tired, otherwise we were in constant motion. Resting now was probably best. I still had to make sure June was going to be ok, and hopefully the paste stopped anything from getting worse for her too. We needed a break.

Between high tensions, arguing, and now swarms of biting insects, I don't know how I'm going to survive if things don't improve.

I'll figure it out, I guess...

CHAPTER 20

June and Leo had gone back to their usual banter, but this time it was all in good fun. This came as a relief to me. June was in much better spirits, and the redness of the beetle bites had lessened. I had reapplied a new layer of paste before beginning our day. Most importantly though, the three of us were getting along. I don't know how we'd get through any of this if we couldn't manage that!

"Knock, knock," June began.

"Who's there?" I asked with a laugh.

My best friend continued the joke by saying, "Yul."

"Yul who?" Leo added in.

"Yul never know…" June whispered, making me and Leo laugh.

The tunnels had become less terrifying in the past day or so. At least I think it has been a day? We only took one real break to rest, so that's how I decided to count it. It's so hard to tell since it's always dark. Walking through the tunnels however, has become more enjoyable since my friends started to get along, and no more bug encounters.

We finally came upon something different within the

tunnels; an intersection. There was one path that went forward, one that went right, and one that went left. It was the first real branch point that veered off the straight line. I was prepping my ribbon to tie as a marker while Leo and I discussed which way we should go. June was strangely silent, as if she were listening to something.

"Julia, Leo," she said nervously, catching our attention, "I think I hear something."

Leo and I became silent as well, trying to listen to what June may have heard. We then realized she was right. Somewhere in the tunnels, there was a whisper that echoed throughout the narrow cave.

"Hello!" the voice rang out, bouncing across all of the walls in front of us. Gradually, as it became louder, closer, and clearer, we were able to differentiate that it was coming from the far right tunnel. I quickly attached my ribbon and we cautiously proceeded in that direction. We were rounding the second corner when we suddenly came into view of the most unexpected creature.

Stepping out from the shadows stood a young girl, probably about 16 or 17 years old, who was wearing a dress made of rags and holding a lantern. Her light brown hair was all tangled and messy, and she was covered in filth. Through the dirt and grime, I noticed the most unique markings. On one side of her face she had a discoloration that began at her ear and stretched randomly across her jawline. It was a discoloration that was part of her actual skin. She was smiling to greet us, ignorant of her appearance or any irregularity we may have noticed.

"It's been a long time since I had visitors!" the girl said excitedly, "I'm Elizabeth, but you can just call me Beth!"

"Um...I'm Julia, and these are my friends Leo and June," I slowly replied, "Nice to meet you."

"Follow me!" Beth exclaimed, motioning for us to come with her down the path going forward, "This is the path to continue."

Hesitantly, the three of us started to walk towards her. Curiously, June asked, "Why are you down here?"

"Oh, I've always been down here," She answered, "My father visits me, and when I ask him why he keeps me here, he always says it's for my safety."

"What do you do down here all by yourself?" I asked.

"Oh, I mostly read." she answered.

"You have access to books?" I questioned her, surprised anyone living in a maze of tunnels could even read.

"Yes, my father taught me how to read," Beth responded, "And he brings me books every time he visits me. My current favorite is a book called the Dictionary!"

"That's...nice," Leo slowly replied, trying his best to be sincere to the girl. "What has been your favorite word so far?" he asked her.

"Oh, I have two favorite words. The first begins with the letter B. It's bamboozle. Try it. Isn't it so fun to say?"

she asked this while beginning to repeat the word over and over to herself. I couldn't help but to smile at the sweet innocent attitude that this girl was just dripping with.

"What's the other word?" June chimed in, interrupting the girl's fun.

"Oh, the other word starts with the letter M. Murder!" she said very mysteriously while she slowly directed her gaze straight at June. I glanced at Beth again, forcing myself to reevaluate my initial impression. I was going to have to keep a much closer eye on her.

Leo did his best to ignore this last piece of information and wisely asked, "Hey, so do you know where this tunnel leads us?"

She replied, "Oh you know, this way or that way. There's no real way to know for sure."

For a minute, we walked in silence. That was the least helpful answer she could've given us. All three of us glanced confused, uncertain looks at each other. Can we really trust directions from this very strange girl? Is this actually the way we need to be going? And also, for that matter, how does she even know where we are on route to? We began attempting to discreetly whisper to each other, creating some additional space between us and the girl.

I attempted asking both of them, "What do you think? Should we try to leave her, and backtrack? I don't have a good feeling about her."

Before either of them could respond, Beth stopped walking and turned to face me.

"That's a very pretty ribbon you have there!" Looking at the white ribbon that was attached to my pack, she commented, "Can I touch it? Can I have some for my hair?"

"No!" I said, backing slowly away from her, "It is very important for our journey. I really can't risk running out of any."

"Oh, I see," She replied, disappointed, "I'm sorry."

"It's fine," I sighed, resigning to give her a piece, "I use it to tag our route through the tunnels so we won't get lost. But it would make a pretty hair bow."

"Well, thank you," Beth responded, happily receiving the piece of ribbon, and then quickly changed the subject by asking, "Wanna know another thing about me?"

"Why not?" June added.

"I have to take this weird medicine every day," She said, "It's only been a few days now, but it always makes me feel kinda dizzy. I don't know exactly why I have to take it, but father said I should, so I do. He's my father after all."

"Have you thought about quitting the medication?" Leo asked.

"Oh, I have, but if I did, father would yell at me for disobeying him. He says I am sick and that this medicine will cure me," the girl answered. Her innocence made me reevaluate her yet again. She was physically a teenager, but she behaved more like a young girl.

I needed to know more so I asked, "Beth, you've lived in the tunnels your whole life? How have you managed?"

"My dad comes, of course!" She answered like it was the most obvious answer ever. "Would it be ok if I walk with you some more?"

"Well, I guess that would be ok. Do you have any idea as to where this tunnel may lead?" I questioned her again while glancing back and forth to Leo and June.

"I'm not sure. My father doesn't want me to wander off because he says it's not safe and safety is the most important thing," she singsang out to us. The now four of us walked forward as Beth could not help but continue her storytelling. The girl had a lot to say, or was just not used to having other people around to talk to.

"My dad once brought me a book about a girl and a wizard and witches, and a path. We could be the people in that book! I'm the girl, and you can be the nice witch," she stated, looking at me.

"And you can be the wicked witch," she said, snarkily at June.

"Lion," she ended with as she smiled looking up at Leo.

She began to link our arms and skip happily down the tunnel. I knew exactly what book she was referring to, but my friends looked completely confused. They looked more like they were being dragged further into a dark hole. I couldn't help but laugh at the entire exchange.

"This seems like a good place to stop for a bit," June abruptly stopped and as such, unlinked arms. Beth was very displeased with this and she was sticking to the character attributes she had placed on all of us.

"Ow! What did you do that for!" June yelled out grabbing Leo's and my attention. She was standing addressing Beth who was staring very smugly back at June.

"She pulled my hair!" June added.

"Well, I thought I saw something in it. My mistake." Beth innocently responded. Oh goodness, I couldn't help but roll my eyes at what was now happening between these two. June has been especially unlucky lately.

"Let's be careful then Beth. We don't want to hurt anyone," I tried my best to softly correct her. June glared at me and I could tell she was instantly annoyed that I was favoring Beth in this instance.

"You know my father. He says I should protect myself, if I need to. I don't think I know any of you particularly well. Maybe I should defend myself against all of you!" she stated aggressively. I was automatically caught a bit off guard. Her features had completely shifted, and an expression of distrust blanketed her face. Her posture and stance had shifted as well, and it looked like she might become violent at any moment.

"I thought we were becoming friends," Leo sweetly addressed her. She only glared at him, squinting her eyes in thought.

"You might be the ok one. Maybe. But definitely not her," she stated as she pointed aggressively at June. June looked unnerved by the undeserved hatred that was spewing her way. She remained quiet, which was incredibly smart on her part. There was nothing she could do or say that would've changed her mind.

"It's been a long day. Maybe we are all just a bit tired and should rest for the day." I chimed in, hoping to calm her down.

"I think I've had enough fun for today. I'm not staying here with you," Beth decided to inform us. I couldn't help but think this was rather odd. I definitely didn't feel right about leaving her behind, but I wasn't sure how to convince her to do something that clearly disobeyed her father's rules. She proceeded to march in the opposite direction, her footsteps becoming quieter and quieter as she disappeared into the darkness.

CHAPTER 21

It was the next day, after the Beth encounter, and Leo was still obsessing over the girl and her supposed story. Currently, he was fixated on investigating the medications she claimed to take.

"Maybe the medicine made Beth act aggressively? One minute she seemed so sweet and innocent and the next, she was wanting to start a fight," Leo commented curiously.

June sighed, "Can you please talk about something else now, Leo?"

"Fine..." Leo muttered grumpily. For the next few minutes, the three of us continued to walk in silence. Every once in a while, we each separately thought we heard the slightest noise of what sounded like a muffled giggle. We would turn to look back, but to no avail. It was just darkness that surrounded us. It had been a couple interesting days, and the darkness of the tunnels, the feelings of restlessness, and maybe even a bit of claustrophobia were beginning to become apparent. I reached over and grabbed Leo's hand, feeling like we could both use a bit of closeness.

I certainly could not imagine going through this

on my own, so having my two friends with me did give a welcome distraction. We had taken turns leading through the tunnels, only using one lantern at a time, so as to preserve whatever life was left in them. My eyes had adjusted so well to the dimly lit pathway that the idea of being anywhere bright would've hurt my eyes anyways.

Oddly enough, in the distance, beyond the shine of our lantern, I saw a little bit of light coming from within the tunnels.

"Hey," I said, "Is that light? Have we arrived at the Above already!"

"What's the Above?" a question arose out of nowhere from behind us. It was Beth. She had been following us afterall.

"Hi Beth, what a nice surprise!" I managed to greet her. "I thought you weren't able to come with us any further?"

"I snuck away. I was too curious to see what you were going to do next," she paused.

"I wouldn't go that way if I were you…" she warned as she pointed forward.

We all looked in the direction she was pointing and knew that we had no other option but to keep moving forward. We didn't have the option to turn back, and we certainly weren't going to stay and live in the tunnels with her.

"Come on! Let's go!" June exclaimed. Ignoring Beth, she grabbed my wrist and dragged me towards the light. Leo followed behind us, and I yelled out to Beth, "You can come with us if you want to!"

She just stood there and watched as the three of us continued to run toward the light.

When we got to the end of the tunnel it opened up and we found something very surprising. We walked into an enormous cave, which was lit by suspended, hanging lanterns. But this cave was different. This cave was unique, not just because it was strangely lit by lanterns.

The cave had a huge, deep, dark, bottomless pit. It was so deep that even the glow of the lanterns did not outline the floor, so the true depth was a mystery. The path to get across the cavern was broken up by multiple oddly shaped platforms. As June and I were admiring the scene in front of us, Leo walked up beside me.

"I guess this isn't the Above. So, are we gonna have to jump onto those platforms to get across?" Leo asked with a laugh.

"Yep, I think so," I answered nervously. The route to get across appeared dauntingly dangerous and I began to fear for our safety.

"Well, let's go then, people!" Leo smiled, clearly unaffected. or unaware of the risks that lay ahead. He proceeded to jump onto the first platform. He almost slid off of it, and after catching his balance, he yelled out, "It's slippery!"

"Let's be extra careful, then," I instructed the two of them, before jumping to the first platform myself. I landed right next to Leo, and while the platform was rather slippery, I managed to catch my balance fairly easily, compared to my boyfriend.

Nervously, June followed us onto the small platform, her feet slipping and sliding this way and that, all the while screaming like her life was ending. Once she regained her balance, I jumped to the next platform, which was much more sturdy. Then I went to the third and the fourth smoothly, since they weren't as unstable as the first. Leo followed me slowly, slipping on a few parts, but still making it without any real problems. June, on the other hand, was making a huge racket with every step she took. She nearly fell off every single platform before reaching Leo and me!

"Why did you choose to bring her along, Julia?" he asked me, cringing at June's struggles.

"She's my friend!" I yelled at him, slightly offended, "And she's not that useless, anyway! She's part of my support system!"

"More like she needs a lot of support," Leo retorted and continued under his breath, "She's just getting in the way between us."

"Ahem," June awkwardly stated, "I'm so sorry to interrupt this VERY important discussion, but we have other things to attend to, like, umm...THAT for example."

June shakily pointed in the direction opposite of us, so Leo and I turned our heads to see what the next platform was. In front of us, there was only a huge abyss on the way to the exit. Instead of additional platforms that outlined our way, a single, rather frail looking rope bridge connected the platform we currently were standing on to the other side, requiring us to risk the crossing.

Leo sighed, and then started to say, "Do we have to-"

"Yes, we have to cross using the bridge!" I snapped at him, "Sorry, I meant to say, yes, we have to use the bridge to cross the cavern and escape."

June began to become noticeably more nervous, so I rushed over to comfort her.

Pulling her into a large hug, I softly told her, "Everything will be alright! You'll survive, because I'll be protecting you! There's nothing to worry about! We will do it together."

"You promise?" my best friend nervously asked me.

"I promise," I reassured her gently, pulling away from the hug, and turning towards Leo, "I'll go first,"

"What!" Leo exclaimed, "But what if you-"

"I'll be fine," I sternly told him, before looking ahead at the scene ahead of me. I slowly took the first few steps onto the bridge and it began to sway at the slightest of movement. As I continued I yelled back, "I think we are going to have to cross this one at a time! I don't know if it'll handle more weight."

"Ok, we will wait until you make it to the other

side then!" Leo yelled back, his voice echoing in the enormous open cavern.

I continued, holding onto the ropes on either side of me, and concentrated on placing one foot in front of the other. Breathe, step, recover. Breathe, step, recover. Slowly and steadily, trying my best to not look directly below, I progressed towards the other end of the bridge.

"You're doing so great Julia!" June bellowed out encouraging me. Hearing her voice really kept me moving forward. In one final last push, I made my way off of the bridge and onto the ledge, as I heard both June and Leo cheering me on.

"Ok! Who's next? Just take it nice and slow!" I yelled back to them.

Leo was the next to approach the bridge and took a couple of cautious steps. After gaining some confidence, he picked up speed and went at a rather surprisingly quick pace. Within minutes he was proudly standing beside me safe and sound, and of course with the biggest smile of success.

"Ok June! It's your turn! You can do it!" I yelled encouraging her. June looked so incredibly nervous. She was taking the smallest of steps as she approached the beginning of the bridge and then froze.

"Hey, June!" I called out to her, "You alright?"

"Yea!" She yelled back, "But I don't know how to get across without falling!"

Within a few minutes, I had started to pace back

and forth, contemplating what to do to get June over the abyss. Suddenly, an idea sprung in my head, so I stopped pacing and turned towards my friend.

"What if I come back for you and we really do cross together?" I suggested,

"I'm willing to take that risk!" June responded.

Before I began to head back, Leo stopped me, grabbing my hand and asked, "Are you sure? Maybe I should go instead?"

I looked into his eyes and saw the fear that had swept over him. I knew June trusted me, so I told him, "I'll be fine. It has to be me since I weigh less. I'll be careful."

Smiling at him, he released my hand. I took off my pack and left it behind at his feet. Feeling much lighter, I began to cross the bridge just as I had done before, but arrived back to June in much less time.

"Hold onto my waist," I instructed, "Make sure to just watch where you place each foot one at a time. We are not going to fall when we work together."

After she nodded in response, I felt June's hands on my waist, and we proceeded to slowly cross the bridge.

"Are you doing ok back there?" I asked, checking in since she was unusually quiet.

"Yea, I'm just really concentrating," she managed to reply in her still very nervous voice.

"You're almost here. Just a few more steps!" Leo yelled, his voice pulling us forward.

Eventually, I once again landed next to Leo. June

stood behind me, her eyes closed, still holding onto my waist.

"June," I said softly, "You can let go now. We're safe."

"Really?" She asked, opening her eyes, "Oh, yea. We are safe!"

A moment later, she detached herself from me, and stood up straight next to me. We all turned around to face what we thought to be more tunnels, but instead, we were met with...

"More platforms!" June yelled in surprise, "Oh, come on! Why! I'm not doing those today. Maybe tomorrow! Maybe next week, but not now!"

"Alright, alright!" Leo exclaimed, "We'll rest here! Just calm down!"

Angry at that, June yelled, "I am calm!"

While my two friends got into yet another argument, I began to unpack our things. I set down our sleeping mats and began to eat one of the food bags that I had packed. After I finished eating, I grabbed the ribbon and began making tiny little bows and attached them to the wall, creating a constellation of stars.

"Hey, how are you?" Leo sweetly came up to me, nudging me softly. He had been watching me from his mat, stewing after his altercation with June.

"Oh you know, hanging in there. Not great, but I guess it could always be worse?" I said, forcing a very weak smile. He put his arm around me and tried his best to comfort me, "You can always talk to me, about anything. I'm here for you. We will figure all of this out and get you to the Above, I promise."

We both stared at the ribbons that were scattered against the wall, and I felt comfort in his arms. We went and laid down on our mats, tired from yet another exhausting day. Before I allowed my eyes to close, I took another moment to stare at my newly created stars. Seeing them before me, I couldn't help but think of my dad. I wondered what he was doing at this exact moment, and if I was also in his thoughts. My dad is going to find these ribbon made stars, and be one step closer to finding me too. June and Leo were already trying to sleep, as it was, yet again, a very long, intense day. I turned the lanterns glow to barely a flicker, and curled up as well, in between my friends, and I fell fast asleep on the cold, stone floor.

CHAPTER 22

"Good morning, everybody!"

The voice rang in my ears as I slowly opened my eyes. In the middle of the room, June stood proud and tall, or at least as tall as she could. A wide grin was spread across her face as she looked down on me and Leo.

"5 more minutes…" the boy next to me muttered, rolling onto his side.

"That's no way to start a day, Leo," she said enthusiastically, "Come on! Let's get moving! We still have the second part of the obstacle course to complete! Get up!"

"Is that what we're calling it now?" Leo mumbled. Continuing to grumble, Leo and I got up and started packing our sleeping mats. June just watched us go about this while eating something she had packed.

Once we all finished eating and packing our things, we turned our attention to the platforms ahead of us. They all looked pretty sturdy and easy to cross, unlike the platforms from the day before.

"Well, this should be pretty easy," Leo said, voicing my thoughts.

"Mhmm…" I added on.

June was the one to jump to the platforms first this time. And then she jumped to the second. And then the third. When she got to the fourth platform, she stopped to wait for Leo and I to catch up. We quickly followed behind her footsteps.

Within a few minutes, we had easily crossed to the last platform without much problem. Leo made the final jump over to the ledge that connected back into the tunnels, and I smoothly followed him. June was last to jump, and as she landed next to me, she stumbled quite a bit. She ended up running right into me, pushing me backwards a step. Unfortunately, that step led me straight off the edge of the platform.

Before I knew it, I was barreling down into the dark abyss, falling to my death. My arms reached out, trying to grab hold of anything. I managed to briefly grab some rock formations on the cavern wall and slowed my fall before finally coming to a sudden stop when I hit a tiny ledge.

I landed with a painful thud, but was thankful to have solid rock underneath me as I assessed the damage. My arms and knees were scraped, and there was a gash along my chin that was clearly also bleeding. I stood, looking up above me and saw that getting back up was not going to be simple. I hoisted myself up more firmly, and searched for crevices or any indentations along the wall in front of me. I was able to place my left foot on another ledge on the wall, and began feeling out where to take the next step up. As I began to balance myself, I heard Leo's voice screaming down towards me, "Are you alright, Julia!?"

"I'll be fine!" I yelled back catching my breath, looking upwards to see his face. Leo looked extremely concerned, scared, and even a little...angry too? June stood next to him, looking rather guilty and afraid.

Tightening my grip on the ledge, I began to climb up the cavern wall. It came surprisingly easy to me since I had routinely scaled the tall bookcases in the library to get to higher shelves. Although I had never seen it done, I had managed to read about the activity of rock-climbing from old books in the private section, and this also proved useful now.

While climbing the bookshelves back home was the closest comparison, this actual cavern proved to be very different and much more difficult. I had to reach and stretch myself in very awkward ways to keep moving. There were too many times where I almost fell, and the bag on my back was definitely weighing me down. I'm just glad it didn't fall off when I fell into the abyss. Otherwise, I would've lost a ton of important supplies.

I was almost to the top when everything became completely smooth. The face of the rock was unclimbable. I was starting to feel my muscles tremble at the sheer exertion required to climb. Leo saw my dilemma and got down on his stomach, trying to reach for my hand so I could grab onto him instead. I heard him yell to June, "Grab my legs! Just in case!"

At that, June disappeared from my view, but it was still of no use. His hand was just out of reach. I still continued to feel for anything in the wall I could possibly grip. At about waist high, I came across a tiny crack. I wondered...

I managed to slide my dagger out and slice it directly into the crack leaving all but the handle exposed. I yelled up to Leo, "I'm going to try and step up so I can grab you!" He was ready for it, so I brought my leg up and around, and stepped as firmly as I could, at the same time clasping my hand into Leo's. As the blade bore my full weight it began to crack, and as Leo began to pull me up, the handle flung down and spiraled away below me.

By the time I made it to the top, I was utterly exhausted. Leo and June both had managed to pull me up over the ledge, helping me to my feet. As soon as I was standing, the adrenaline of the life or death situation finally caught up to me, and I realized what had just happened. I had nearly died.

"Are you hurt?" Leo worriedly asked me, interrupting me from my thoughts.

"I'm alright," I tried to reassure him, dusting myself off and noticing that I was actually still bleeding.

"Luckily," he sighed in relief, "You could've died! Isn't that right, June."

June was still standing in the exact same place as before, but now she looked like she was going to cry.

"I'm so sorry, Julia!" June sobbed, "This was all my fault! You could've died just because of my clumsiness!"

"Yea, it is your fault," Leo responded, rage filling his eyes, "She could be dead right now all because of your carelessness!"

Leo continued to yell at my best friend, who was crying her eyes out, and I felt helpless. I had taken out my knife and started slicing off bits of fabric from my sleeves and tied them off to bandage my scrapes as best I could.

Listening to them, I realized I had always known how to make the two of them get along, but now, I had no idea what to do to resolve this. I didn't want to be here with them anymore. Maybe I shouldn't have brought anyone along with me on my task after all. Leo and June have done nothing but slow me down on my quest to help the community of the Underground. All they ever did was argue and argue and argue, yet rarely ever actually help me. Yes, I really cared about them, and we have all grown close, but that does not justify me sticking by their sides. This was my task, and my task alone. My exhaustion and stress could not take the two of them on anymore. Maybe I should just...leave. Walk away. It's probably for the best. So I did. I started walking down the tunnels, tears welling up in my eyes. I could get over these emotions. I could move on. I had to be strong. For the Underground.

That was when I fell into a hole. A deep hole in the ground.

As I was falling, all I could hear was the sound of my

own screams.

CHAPTER 23

When I opened my eyes, I was alone in a dark, stiflingly hot room. I can't believe I fell, again. At least the bottom wasn't that far this time, and the landing wasn't as painful. As soon as I began to observe my surroundings, I looked directly above from where I had fallen. How will my dad ever find me down here? At the same time overhead I heard a high-pitched scream, just before a familiar person landed right on top of me, knocking me back to the floor.

"Oh my god!" June shrieked, still on top of me, "Are you okay, Julia!?"

"Yea, I'm-"

Before I could finish my sentence, another person landed on top of both me and June. Leo. June quickly pushed him off the two of us before getting up herself and offering a hand towards me. Instead of accepting her help like I normally would, I got up on my own, ignoring her, her actions, and her reactions.

Looking around, I saw there was only one way forward and that was a long, narrow hallway with a small orange glow at the end of it. I slowly began to walk down the hall, Leo and June carefully following behind me.

When the three of us reached the end of the hall, we were met with something incredibly shocking. The ground of the cave in front of us was filled with small pools of bubbling lava. I had read about lava, and knew that the center of the Earth was lava, also known as magma. I also knew that if anything even slightly touched it, it would cause major burns. Even the air smelled differently, and it was thick, making it harder to breathe normally.

"What is that!" June exclaimed, "It's so bright and pretty! And...really warm, too!"

"Do not touch it, or even get close to it," I warned her, "Unless you want to get burnt to a crisp, that is."

Instantly, June went silent, trying to shrink herself behind Leo, who looked very apprehensive about whether he should move forwards into the room full of lava, or back to the hall behind us.

"This doesn't seem very safe," he whispered hesitantly.

"Well, we can't go back now, can we?" I replied slightly annoyed.

Carefully, I stepped beside one of the lava pools, and slowly walked around it, trying not to come into contact with the fiery liquid. The cavern air was full of smoke, causing June, who was following behind me, to begin to cough very loudly. Leo, then, began to walk towards us on the path across the room.

We made it past most of the pools before June stopped in her tracks and started coughing like crazy. Leo ran up to her, and held her shoulder with one hand to help support her. Then, he began to cough as well, causing him to move his other arm to his face to block out the smoke. I tried my best to cover my own mouth and nose with my arm.

Within a minute, we were all hunched over coughing from the smoke and light-headed from the heat. My best friend looked like she was going to pass out at any moment from the immense heat.

"We need to keep moving," I instructed through coughs and ragged breathing, "Or else we're not gonna make it through this."

They began to slowly stumble around the next pool of lava, coughing a distressingly long while. By the time we made it to the beginning of the last pool, I felt as though I would pass out any second from the heat.

About halfway past the last pool of lava, I heard the footsteps behind me halt. I turned around carefully, and Leo stood bracing my best friend's body, who was leaning closer and closer, inching towards the lava pool directly beside her. She was unconscious.

I shot Leo a questioning glance, and he responded, "She fainted."

I nodded before turning around and continuing to stumble towards the exit. I knew Leo would be able to carry June across without problem, so I left him to complete that on his own.

Within a few minutes, I was out of the cave, on the ground gasping for the now clear air. Soon enough, I was joined by Leo, who was cradling June's unconscious body against his chest. I don't really understand why, but a strange feeling came into my heart when I saw him hold her like that. It didn't feel like a good emotion, either. I should be grateful that Leo caught June before she fell into lava and burned to death, not...whatever this was.

"Let's walk a bit further, to be safe," he suggested panting heavily, so we began to walk forward. As we were walking, he asked, "Are you alright, Julia?"

I just nodded, and kept walking down the long, endless hall, not even bothering to smile.

Leo was starting to struggle with carrying the weight of June. He hadn't yet recovered his breathing either. Looking at them, I couldn't help but feel bad for both of them.

"Leo, let's stop here for a minute. You need to catch your breath. And we both could use some water, " I said as I grabbed a bottle from my pack.

"Yea, that's a good idea," Leo agreed while setting June gently on the ground between us.

"I wish I knew if June was going to be okay," he said, quite concerned for her. She hadn't stirred at all, but she was breathing. I hadn't even really considered what we would do if one of us seriously got hurt, or something worse. I should've. I am the one who almost died falling into the abyss. We really didn't come prepared enough, and no one even attempted to prep us for what this journey was going to entail. Anger started to rise up in me and I couldn't help but place blame on everyone and everything that may have possibly put me in this situation.

"Leo, this isn't right. This isn't how it should be. We keep getting hurt, or almost dying, or I don't even know!" my voice trailed off in utter desperation.

"Julia, you can't give up. June will recover very soon, you'll see. And then she can go back to annoying both of us again, just like old times," he grinned, trying his best to cheer me up.

Although part of me appreciated the attempt, it failed and my mood remained unaltered. He clearly wasn't understanding what I had meant. He was making light of the seriousness we faced every single second we remained in these tunnels. None of us have a clue what is around the bend, or who or what we may encounter at any moment. Tears started to swell up but I pushed them away, far far, away. There is no time for tears or feeling sorry for myself. I needed to remain strong and push forward, even if the risks are increasingly high.

"I think we should keep moving," I suggested to Leo, ensuring my voice remained solid. Leo nodded in acknowledgment and carefully picked the peaceful looking June back into his arms. The three of us continued down the tunnel, with no looking back.

CHAPTER 24

At the end of the passage, we came to a deadend. Above us a rope ladder hung in the center of an otherwise completely enclosed space, leading upwards into the darkness. For a few minutes, Leo and I debated how we could manage to get a still unconscious June up the long rope. I was trying my best to convince him that he should stay behind with June, while I kept going on my own. He would not agree to this idea at all. June was still in Leo's arms, a fact that I was trying my best to overlook and ignore. I was concerned for her of course, and wanted her to recover, but we were both uncertain about how long it would take for her to wake up. Looking at her just then, we heard a strange breathing noise coming from June herself. The odd sound turned into a loud sneeze and within a second, all of a sudden, she was awake. Blinking, June looked at me, and then Leo.

"You are a weird person," Leo commented, and June turned her head away from him.

"Put me down," she responded coldly, "Now."

Before I could see the rest of the exchange, I turned away from them both and began to climb up the ladder. Seconds later, I heard chattering behind me, alerting me that the other two were following behind.

I made it to the top of the rope without any significant difficulty and found myself looking down yet another long passageway. This passageway was different. Throughout our journey thus far, we had been seeing the same types of markings on the rock walls. In this section of the tunnel however, the markings were clearly now arrows, pointing in the direction I was headed. The arrows were all painted in a rusty red hue, but were large and prominent enough to make out. It was intriguing and I decided to proceed in this direction alone. It was quite a long time before the scenery on the path changed, but when it did, it was major. The hard, stone walls, floor, and ceiling disappeared, and it instead turned lush with greenery. The ceilings were concealed by leaves and trees and the darkness dissipated. The floor was covered in various grasses, vines, and moss. Everything had a blue iridescent glow to it. My skin glowed, and the plants swayed in rhythm to this magical lighting. It must have been some sort of bioluminescence. I decided to stop briefly to attach a ribbon to a large branch overhead...just in case.

"What is this place?" June asked, catching up to me.

Thinking, I remembered a place that had been described in many, many books in the library.

"It's a forest," I answered softly, stopping in place, admiring all of the nuances we were experiencing. You could hear the sound of water rushing in the distance, and tiny water droplets fell onto us from above. The blue haze reflected the deep, rich coloring of the plants that surrounded us. There were tiny flying insects that would project a light from their bodies and they were scattered throughout the treeline, shimmering like blinking stars. The leaves were so dense that I began to use my remaining dagger as a means to clear a path.

"It's beautiful," Leo commented as we made our way deeper into the folds of the forest.

Taking a moment to rest from slicing through the brush, I heard a rustle in the leaves. Quickly, I pulled out my hatchet from the satchel on my waist. Then I heard another rustle, and then another. There seemed to be something or someone circling the three of us. We huddled together looking for the source of this noise.

Briefly, I looked forward, debating if I should just keep moving, when I heard June scream very loudly behind me. Looking back, I saw a blue, feathered creature attacking her face.

June must have screamed so loudly that it startled the animal and it flew away, landing on the branch of a nearby tree. Studying its features, I recognized what kind of creature it was. I had read about birds many times before, but had never seen one in person.

This bird was very large, about the size of my head, and had bright, blue feathers. Its beak was large, and its talons were long and sharp. Recalling a book I read specifically on birds, I could remember this bird was called a macaw.

Reaching into my bag, I pulled out a piece of bread and broke off a bit of the crust. Then, I laid my hand a safe distance away from the bird's beak. The animal eyed me directly, slowly moved forward to take the bread, and then stretched its wings out to go into flight. It circled around me a couple times before landing on my shoulder, bringing the first real smile to my face in days.

"Aww!" June exclaimed, "That's cute! Do you think it's friendly?"

"I don't know," I responded, "But it seems to like me, for some weird reason."

"That's nice!" Leo grinned, reaching his hand out towards the bird on my shoulder, "Come to me, pretty thing! Ow-"

The beautiful, elegant macaw...really enjoyed biting people. The bird didn't bite me once, but for the next few minutes, it had a field day ruining the attitudes of my two companions. It was so funny that I ended up rolling on the ground laughing, while the other two were being tortured by a bird!

"You should name it Snapper!" Leo shouted, trying to avoid the feathered creature, but failing.

"Hmm..." I sat up and thought for a few minutes, before getting a better idea, "I actually like the name Diamond! Because the diamond is a very pretty jewel, and she looks like a female bird deserving of the same beautiful name!"

Grumbling at my response, Leo went back to his epic battle with the bird. It only truly ended when I managed to call her over to rest on my shoulder again.

"I think we should rest here," I instructed, "It seems safe, and look! Fruit trees!"

We hadn't had anything fresh in such a long time, it felt like a real special treat. I reached up and picked what looked like a large lemon, or orange. I had never seen such a strange looking fruit. Slicing it in half proved right in that it was nothing like I had seen before. I took the first bite and the juicy, floral flavors ran down my throat. I sliced a piece for Diamond and she also happily swallowed the delicious fruit. June and Leo began to do the same, although slightly side-eying Diamond the entire time. Feeling content to have reached such a beautiful spot, we decided to settle in for the day.

I silently wandered off a little, while June and Leo were setting up for the night. With Diamond in tow, I was drawn towards the sound of flowing water. She flew ahead, as if knowing the destination I seeked, and was asking me to follow. She ended up settling on a low branch of a tree, completely covered with white blossoms. Beyond it, a waterfall trickled down the face of the rock wall. The source was so high that it was impossible to look directly up to see where it began. Only a tiny white hole of light was above, and the walls gradually became wider and wider into the cavern.

The water was so pure you could see through to the bottom, and the rocks beneath sparkled like gems. They were all different colors; shades of purples, greens, blues. It was so magical I could not resist reaching down and touching the surface. The water rippled beneath my touch, and it was refreshingly cool. I cupped my hands and brought some to my mouth and the taste was so pure it was like I had never experienced drinking water before this moment. I saw my reflection in the clear pool and proceeded to splash my face with this seemingly holy water, instantly removing the days worth of dirt, sweat, and blood that had caked on my face.

Glancing around me, appreciating the fact that I was still alone, apart from Diamond who was still watching over me from the nearby tree, I decided to undress and wade into the clear waters. I had no idea how deep it truly became, but the idea of floating on my back, if only for a little bit, was too overwhelming. Stepping into the water, I instantly felt relief and the stress of my journeys temporarily washed away. I let the water flow over me, and I purposefully plunged my entire self under, holding my breath and embracing the absolute quiet I found beneath. This was the most magical place, and to have found this respite in the midst of such turmoil was beyond welcome. Losing track of time, and rather begrudgingly, Diamond and I made our way back to the camp where Leo and June must have been waiting.

As we approached the camp, I heard muffled screams.

It was Leo and June calling for help! I couldn't make out which direction their voices echoed from. I would head in one direction, it would stop, and then I would hear it from elsewhere. I began yelling back, hoping my voice would carry to reach them. Diamond was actually what led me to them. They were trapped.

CHAPTER 25

June and Leo were caught in a large rope net hanging from the branch of a massive tree. Their faces were instantly relieved when they saw me come out of the brush to find them.

"What happened? Are you both ok?" I asked rather worriedly.

"I think so, it caught us by surprise!" June bellowed down from above me.

"Do you think you can cut us down?" Leo asked. I walked around the entirety of the net trying to assess the situation and how best to retrieve them. One way or another, they were going to have a long, hard fall.

Warning them I told them, "I think I can throw my hatchet at the branch and it will cut the rope free. You are going to fall a really long way though! Do you think you'll be able to handle it?"

"Anything to get us out of here! Just do it!" June yelled back. I walked back a few paces, lined up my sights and threw. It was a perfect shot, and within seconds they came barreling down, landing quite hard onto the ground. They managed to get up, and although a little bruised up, they seemed ok. I, myself, was a little concerned because my hatchet was now stuck in the tree, at a height that was impossible to recover. Losing my hatchet, but saving my friends was an automatic decision and a correct one.

"That was really strange. We are going to have to be really careful. Clearly there are hidden traps through here," Leo advised.

As we were about to make our way back to our camp, we heard more movement nearby. Out of the brush a very thin old man appeared. He began to shuffle slowly towards us, his hand trembling as he clutched a wooden cane that was carved into a spear at the top of it. As he came into view, I noticed how bony his features were and how unfocused his eyes appeared as he gazed in our direction. His clothing looked as if it was an accumulation of rags collected year after year. There was something unsettling about him, and we stood undecidedly as he continued to slowly move towards us; the only sound was the echoing of his cane as it was tapped across the floor in rhythm with his steps.

There was a mist that began to envelope us, and tiny water droplets began to fall onto us. I couldn't help but wonder if this is what rain is like...at the same time slightly unsure of what to expect from this man who stood hunching before us. He was the first to speak.

"Did you all find yourself in trouble?" he asked, noticing the broken net that was underneath our feet. "I'm awfully sorry about that. You managed to get tangled up into one of my animal traps. Well, no matter. I'll just have to repair it now, and I'll have to find some more rope somewhere…"

He continued to trail off in thought, most of what he said was either inaudible or unintelligible. Leo stepped forward, shielding June and I from this strange looking man.

"So, you live here? In the forest then?" Leo asked him.

"Oh, no. Not in the forest. I have a cabin down that way," he answered while pointing in the direction of another tunnel. He paused and then continued, "I am so sorry. Where are my manners? You all are just passing through so I should be more hospitable. My name is Franklin, but I go by Frank. Nice to meet you."

He gave us a lowly bow, widely grinning.

Leo continued to address the man solely, "Hello, my name is Leo, and these are my friends."

He motioned behind him, but was clearly not comfortable giving out any further information about us, which I was totally ok with.

"You can't stay here in the forest, not with all these creatures roaming around here, especially at night," he waved his free arm in the air gesturing to the darkened space above us, "You need to come with me of course. I will give you a warm room and some food. I bet you all are hungry, tired of eating that packaged stuff I bet."

He was eyeing our packs as if he knew exactly what was contained in each and every one of them.

"Come on then. I don't have all night," he continued to mutter to himself as he began to head in the direction of the tunnel towards his home.

I was beyond conflicted. I was definitely curious to be sure, but also very apprehensive and cautious. I could tell Leo didn't like the idea one bit, and June was clinging to me, awaiting to follow whatever decision either of us came to. I took the initiative. I'm not afraid of an old man who can barely move and probably can't even see straight. I began to follow behind, catching one last sight of Diamond as she was perched in a nearby tree before leaving the forest, and Leo and June joined right instep.

Frank muttered to himself the entirety of the short distance from the forest to his mysterious looking cabin. We didn't even think to interrupt this inner banter, and so quietly followed behind; a safe distance behind, just in case. The tunnel led us to a strange, little wooden cabin built into the tunnel wall. And through its windows, there was light. Not artificial light, like back in the Underground, but natural light. Fire. Not only that, but there was movement inside. Another person? I couldn't believe my eyes.

Frank bellowed out as we approached the cabin, "Oliver, come out here! We've got guests! Come welcome them!"

The door opened and a young man around my age appeared. He was a little taller than Leo, and it looked as though he hadn't brushed his long hair in weeks.

Another noticeable feature was that one of his eyes was barren and opaquely white, making him partially blind. His clothes were an average Underground outfit, just with more dirt, grime, stains, and holes.

As we reached the entrance, he stared down right at me with his one, actually functioning eye, his mouth hanging slightly ajar. Who was this guy?

We all nodded towards him as we passed him and entered this mysterious cabin. Inside, we saw a single room in front of us. A small, round, wooden table with 4 wooden chairs was off to the side of the room. There was a sofa with a woolen blanket and pillow, most likely doubling as a bed, and a cot in the corner. Directly in front of the sofa was a real, wood fireplace that was currently filling the small space with warmth and light. It was just as I had always imagined, except even better. I could not help myself as I just stared blankly into the colorful flames that flickered before us. A real fire. I couldn't wrap my head around it. Real fire, with real wood! How did he get real wood in here?

There were also cabinets in the corner of the room, and one of the cabinet doors was open, revealing containers of food. How did this guy get fresh food and water? How is that even possible down here in the tunnels!?

As we stood awkwardly in the middle of the room, Oliver moved what must have been his things off the sofa, and motioned for us to sit down. So we did. I sat in between my two companions, Oliver sat on the floor, and Frank dragged over one of the wooden dining chairs before falling into it.

"Well isn't this nice," Frank continued, "Which one of you is the chosen one? I know how it works, so you better just speak up now."

"I am," I spoke for the first time since coming into the man's presence. He smiled very slyly and looked pleased with this revelation. He glanced over at Oliver and shared, "Oliver here, he was a Selection winner. He didn't make it to the Above, now did he?"

With that, the old man couldn't help but chuckle to himself. Gazing down at Oliver, I could tell he was very uneasy and uncomfortable with this conversation, or maybe this situation. Perhaps we were invading his space.

I couldn't help myself and asked Oliver, "How long have you been staying here?"

Oliver struggled to find his voice but managed to clear his throat and answered, "I've been living here for an entire year now."

Hearing this, I now remembered him. The previous year, I saw Oliver walk onto the stage as the Counselor announced that he was the chosen one. I saw the horror in his face when he realized he would have to leave the Underground. I clearly remember him having both of his eyes. Something tragic must have happened to him through the tunnels, stranding him and forcing him to remain in this spot. We were going through so many similar circumstances.

Frank interjected with a wide broad smile, "That's right. He was nice enough to stay here with me and help out a weak old man."

Oliver said nothing.

"What about you Frank? How long have you lived here? How did you come to have a cabin here?" Leo asked, surprisingly confident.

"Curious are you, boy? Well, let's see now. I've been here a long time. I was a special chosen one from the Selection too, you see. I was a young man back then, like you! Ha!"

The man laughed at the irony in this but managed to continue, "I don't know about you, but I'm barely keeping my eyes open. How about you Oliver? Are you having trouble keeping that one good eye of yours open?" he teased. Oliver said nothing.

"You three are welcome to lay out along the floor here and stay warm by the fire. It'll surely be warmer here than out there. Choice is up to you."

He left the decision hanging in the air as he limped over to his cot and lied down, his back facing us. Oliver stood up and awaited our decision as well, because we were sitting on his bed.

We each stood up and went to our packs that we had set by the door when we first entered. We set out our mats nearest the fire, stretched out and went to sleep.

CHAPTER 26

I was being shaken. I was being shaken awake. I sat up and saw it was Oliver. The fire was still beautifully lighting the small room, providing an excess of heat. June and Leo were still asleep, and there was a soft snoring sound that was coming from the direction of the cot. Oliver motioned for me to follow him. I got up as quietly as I could, and followed him as he slowly opened the front door. He shut it just as slowly behind us, hearing only a small audible click once it was secure.

"You need to get out of here, today! Now even!" Oliver warned. "You don't know what it's been like for me."

"What do you mean?" I asked, feeling very concerned for his well-being. Before he even had a chance to answer, he withered into himself and backed away from me. Frank had come onto the front porch.

"Well, what do we have here? A little romance brewing Oliver?" he smiled and winked at me.

"No sir, I was just getting the most current gossip from the Underground. You know it's always entertaining to see what those guys are up to," he answered as calmly as he could.

Frank then exclaimed, "Oh fun, I do enjoy those stories too! Ok, let's hear it then, what's the juicy gossip?"

Wow, way to put me on the spot. I couldn't help but hesitate. I had absolutely nothing. My mind was completely blank. I tried my best to quickly recover, if just for Oliver's sake, and made something up to hopefully suffice.

"Well there's a rumor going around," I paused, still trying to formulate my story, "that the community wants to kick the current Counselor out of office. It would be the first time in the entire history of Underground if this were to happen. Apparently, the Counselor is mad with power and people are saying he's literally mentally unstable. He has become violent with the members of the Council and beats them. It's also been said that he wants to introduce torture back into society for anyone who defies him."

I waited to hear if Frank bought the story. The actual story that I had recalled was from reading about a British King who actually did go mad and was overthrown. I felt kinda proud of myself for mixing a history lesson into my life.

"Now, that's quite the rumor! Woohee! What I wouldn't give to be a fly on the wall of that Counselor." Frank exclaimed, as he happily went back inside and started banging things around in the kitchen area of the room. I guess it was morning after all. The disturbance must have woken Leo because he came out to find me on the porch alone with Oliver. He did not look happy.

"Good morning," he addressed me specifically as he leaned over and kissed the top of my forehead. "What are you guys talking about?" Oliver said nothing.

"Oh you know, I was just asking Oliver how he came to live in the tunnels with Frank. I'm sure it's a very interesting story." I added.

"I bet. I would love to hear all about that too!" Leo continued and was about to say more when June appeared in the doorway, half asleep. Her hair was a crumpled mess, and she was fighting to keep her eyes open.

"What's he doing in there? Making so much noise? Doesn't he know I'm still trying to sleep?" June whined to us. I think I'll always find amusement in the fact that she is capable of finding a way to insist that the world around her accommodate her every demand.

"Yea, I know it's hard. At least we were able to sleep somewhere warm for a change. I was beginning to forget what that felt like. And a real fire! That was amazing!" I was really trying to get her to see the positives this morning.

"Breakfast is ready!" Frank called from within. We began to file back into the small room and saw that he had managed to attempt setting the table. Everything was mismatched but sure enough, there were 4 plates, 4 forks, and 4 tea cups all set. Oliver went straight to the sofa and tried his best to stay out of Frank's way.

"I don't know if you know this, but that forest has all types of creatures. If you're lucky, you can catch them just in time and have enough food to last for months! Isn't that right Oliver?" Oliver was ignoring us completely and staring at the floor.

This did not stop Frank from continuing his one sided conversation, "So eat up, we got some real nice quail eggs here. Have you ever had quail eggs? It's a special treat. You just happened to be here at the right time. Oh, I almost forgot, I have a really smooth floral tea."

He managed to raise himself to his feet and hobble over to the fire where he had a kettle hanging directly over the flames of the roaring fire. He proceeded to pour the tea into my cup first and I was immediately hit by the scent of almond.

"What kind of tea did you say this was?" I innocently asked him.

He smiled easily and answered, "I found the root of it in the forest. I think you'll really enjoy the flavor."

As he poured a pale blue liquid into my ivory cup, the bitter scent of almond was undeniable. He had already begun to pour cups for June and Leo. June was lifting the cup to her mouth and I knocked it out of her hand, spilling the contents, and the cup shattered into pieces as it fell onto the floor. Both Leo and June looked surprised and were obviously questioning my thinking.

"Don't drink this tea! It's not safe. I remember reading about the dangers of different toxins found in nature. He's trying to poison us!" I yelled as I rose from the table, my friends rising beside me.

Frank tried to correct me, "Don't be silly. Why would I want to poison my visitors? Now, be a good girl and drink your tea."

"No thank you, sir," I asserted, "We will be leaving now."

"Oh, is that so," he argued, "I don't believe you're going anywhere, missy."

He limped toward me as he began to raise his walking stick, the pointed spear heading straight towards me. Leo and June were directly behind me at this point, and with the room being so small we were backing up against the door. I bent down, grabbing my dagger that was easily reachable from the side pouch and braced for whatever was to happen next. I was ready for this. I had trained for this exact moment. To protect. I am protecting us from him, the threat.

He made jabbing motions in my direction as he got closer and closer. I shielded his direct blow, shoving the stick to the side with my arm and kicking him full on in the gut. He lost his balance and stumbled back onto the floor. The rage in him grew, and you could see the intensity in his eyes as he glared back at me.

"Don't get up. It's best if you stay where you are. I don't want to hurt you!" I warned after him as I saw him attempting to get back to his feet.

He replied with the most forceful, hateful tone, "I

don't know who you think you are little missy, but you need to learn to respect your elders!"

At that he lunged forward, surprising me at his newfound agility. I moved just quickly enough to feel only the slightest scrape of the spear as it slid past my cheek. His momentum was so powerful that he himself rammed into me, knocking me into my friends, and all of us onto the floor. He was lying on top of me.

"Julia, are you ok? Did he hurt you? June, help me get him off of her." Leo instructed June.

As they readied themselves to pull him off of me, I realized my hand was still gripping the handle of my last remaining dagger. I let go as his body slid to the side of me. The dagger had penetrated squarely into his chest. His already foggy eyes were lifeless. I stood up immediately, replaying the events over and over in my head. My hands were shaking, my entire body was trembling, and I was having a hard time controlling my breathing. I needed air. I grabbed for the door handle and urgently left the stiflingly hot cabin.

I paced back and forth, trying to calm down and catch my breath. I looked up to see June and Leo in the doorway watching me, their faces full of concern.

"Julia, you did it. You protected us. You saved our lives." Leo said as he approached me, offering his arms for comfort. I let him embrace me and I could hear his heart beating strongly as my ear rested against his chest. At that moment, I also saw Oliver make his way onto the porch. I had forgotten about Oliver. He looked pale as a ghost, and his expression was impossible for me to make out.

"Oliver, are you ok? I didn't mean for any of this to happen. Please forgive me." I begged him.

He instantly looked at me and reassured me, "Are you kidding? My life has been a nightmare. I never had the strength to stand up to him. I've almost died countless times while in the tunnel, and I thought this was the only way I could remain alive. You have rescued me."

In that moment I could see the fear that had weighed upon him for all of those months lifted away. I felt so sorry for him and I wanted to do more to help. "You should come with us! We can make it to the Above together now!" I exclaimed.

"The tunnels are like a maze. I tried to find the way, but kept finding myself back in the forest." Oliver continued, "There are so many dangers lurking. I don't know if I'm ready to face that again."

"We will be all together. We will keep each other safe!" I begged him. With that he approached me closer, lowering his voice so that June and Leo, who had gone back inside the cabin to begin packing our mats, wouldn't overhear.

"I have some very serious information to give you, Julia," he said, "Just…be ready for the worst, alright?"

I nodded, staring up at him.

"When I was in the Underground, I had heard many stories about the Selection," Oliver started, "I heard that in some cases the Counselor would allow the chosen person to bring two companions along with them. However, these companions were said to always be completely devoted to the Underground. So much so that they would go so far as to even kill for the society if necessary."

"It is said that when the Counselor allows the chosen person to have companions, he is purposefully sending that person to their death."

"What?" the words came out as a shaky whisper, and I took a step backward. I was surely visible through the window of the cabin, but I couldn't help it that my face was plastered in fear.

"You have to be careful with these friends of yours, Julia," he said, "There's a chance they will betray you."

The door opened, and Leo and June came running out of the cabin. Leo grabbed Oliver by his shirt collar and punched him in the face. June held my arm, and was trying to pull me away. But I wouldn't move. I couldn't move. Was Oliver being serious? Is that why Leo punched him?

Leo ran over to me and picked me up with force, causing me to scream and kick on instinct. He put me over his shoulder, and his grip on me was rock solid. I couldn't move, or even breathe.

"Julia! Not that way!" Oliver yelled after us.

Oliver was on his knees, looking up at me with worry and fear, but before I could respond to his call, Leo started moving away, carrying me over his shoulder as he ran. Instantly, everything around me became a blur of light and darkness.

After a little while, Leo finally set me down. And then he had the *audacity* to *smile* at me.

"Alright!" he exclaimed with a grin, "That was close. We almost didn't get out of that one."

Anger was building up in my veins. How could he say that! How could he be so *awful*? I wanted to let him know how I felt, so I did the only thing I could think of.

I slapped him across the face.

CHAPTER 27

"What the hell, Julia!" Leo yelled, "I just saved your life!"

"I don't need your saving!" I screamed, my words full of rage, "There wasn't even any kind of danger!"

"Oliver was clearly not a good person either! You can't trust him!" he shouted, "I was trying to protect you! You're just overreacting."

"Overreacting," my voice got oddly quiet, "How am I overreacting? Are my emotions just invalid to you? Is that what this is about?"

"Julia-"

"And how was Oliver a threat to us? He's basically a similar version of me. If you find him dangerous, do you think the same of me too? And Leo. I don't need your so-called protection. I can take care of myself."

I began to walk away from the two people I thought I could call my friends, and then Leo shouted one last thing to me.

"I love you, Julia!"

"...Leo?" I asked.

"Yes?" he responded.

"Love yourself."

◆ ◆ ◆

I managed to trudge on, with Leo and June trailing
behind. I needed space. I have no idea how to go on. I was
losing hope. At this point all of us were traumatized. Even
now as we walked, we could see a trail of blood on the
ground basically outlining our route. It looked new and
old at the same time, but it was most definitely creating a
stain in the stone beneath our feet.

The three of us followed this blood soaked trail.
What else could we do!? We might run into someone who
was actively bleeding and might be in need of help ahead
of us. At least, this was my hope. Perhaps it was just
wishful thinking.

So we walked. And walked. And walked some
more. Eventually, we decided to stop to rest for a little bit.

"We've been going a long time today. I feel like we
need to find the end of this before we stop for the night. I
wonder where it ends up," Leo said, talking about the trail
of blood, and being extra cautious when speaking to me.

"Yea," I agreed with him, because where could it
possibly lead us to? And how could it possibly be worse
than what we've already left behind?

We sat contemplating in silence, and after a little
while, we painstakingly began to walk again. After
having walked for so long all day, we were surprised
when we had a visitor. It was my first sighting of
Diamond since I last saw her in the forest. She found

me! She began circling above us, and it immediately brightened my mood. It did not help my companions, as they would flinch and complain about the creature.

At one point, Diamond flew down to sit on June's head, but she only ran away from the bird. Diamond most likely saw it as a game, so she chased June around the corner in the tunnel ahead of us. Leo and I could only hear June's scream, until quite suddenly that stopped, and she yelled out to us instead.

"Guys!" she exclaimed, "There may or may not be another hole in the ground up ahead!"

"Is there a way in, out, or around this hole?" I asked as I quickened my pace to catch up to her.

"Yes," June responded, "There are ladders going down on either side. They look pretty sturdy, too."

"That's good at least," Leo commented.

When we turned the corner, we saw Diamond flying in circles around June, who was standing next to a narrow dark opening in the ground. I could clearly see that the ladders very quickly disappeared into the darkness below.

"Well, I guess this is the only way. We better get started," Leo said unenthusiastically, beginning his descent down the ladder.

While Leo descended on one side, I matched him on the other and before long we were standing beside each other at the bottom of the pit. The first thing that hit us, even before we reached the ground, was the strong putrid scent that filled the air. It smelled of rotting meat, or maybe even rotten eggs? All I knew was that I instantly gagged and tried my best to breath through my mouth as I covered my nose. The ground we were standing on was made of a weird substance that seemed both hard and soft, varying in height. It was like walking on a pile of...I'm not even sure. Neither of us could see what it was because of the dim lighting. Our only source of light was the lantern I held.

When June stepped off the ladder, her shoes made a crunching sound on the floor. She made a disgusted face, reaching down to the ground to see what the strange substance was. When she brought her hand back into the light, all three of us were absolutely terrified.

In her hand was a human skull, covered in hundreds of tiny black beetles.

My entire body tensed, and it felt as though I really was going to throw up. The floor beneath my feet was made of bones, crushed bones, bodies, decomposing bodies, blood, liquids. The soft squishy parts must have been flesh and muscle, and the hard spots were bone. I couldn't move, couldn't breathe. The skull made a crunch when it fell back to the ground out of June's hand, her skin still had remnants of the dried blood-soaked bone from where she picked it up.

Skin. My imagination gets the best of me and I could not stop visualizing skin beneath me as well. Clinging to me. A lost wandering soul, reaching, wishing to escape this cruel place.

It was horrible. Absolutely horrible.

"Julia," a voice came from my right, startling me. But when I turned, it was just Leo.

"Yes?" I whispered, my voice shaky.

"Do we keep moving, or what?" he nervously asked me.

"Yea," I replied, "Let's keep moving."

I tried to stay calm as I walked through the piles of bodies. I really tried, and it was really difficult. I could tell that Leo was having an equally hard time staying composed. June, however, didn't try hiding her fear.

She screamed in horror whenever there was a crunch under our feet. She gagged when she felt the soft, squishy substances underneath her while walking. Her breathing was so heavy that someone a million miles away would be able to hear her terror.

June never liked to hide how she felt. I had known that ever since I met her, so seeing her now, I really shouldn't have been surprised.

After what felt like an eternity, we made it across this bone yard to another ladder that would hopefully get us up and out of this nightmare. Leo went first, Diamond flying up with him and landing on his shoulder when he reached the top safely. I let June go up next. As she was climbing I turned to look behind my shoulder at the now completely pitch black room.

How did all these dead bodies get in here?

How did all of them end up dead?

Is this what happened to all the other people chosen at the Selection?

I couldn't help but feel that Frank had something to do with this pit. I just couldn't shake it. My entire body wanted to eliminate the intrusive thoughts that kept pushing their way back in. Is this where we would have ended up?

I climbed up the ladder to join my companions, and we walked away from the hidden horrors behind us, leaving behind those horrible thoughts along the way.

CHAPTER 28

I was done. We were all reaching our breaking points. After trying to sleep, and failing as the nightmares of the entire day consumed me, I decided to go off alone. This was my quest, and I didn't need them preventing me from completing it the way I wanted to. I had been walking for a while. When I first left the other two, I was running. I couldn't let them catch up to me, so I ran. At one point, I ran into a part of the tunnels that had already been marked by a ribbon. I just continued to follow it until I reached a different intersection. I specifically chose a different route this time to avoid running into Leo and June, who I am now certain were following me. It was worthless to try and mark my route at this point, as I had already given up hope that my dad would be able to follow my route. I knew that if I made it out of here alive, I would have to be the one to come back and somehow get to him. Instinctively, I veered off to the right, and have been walking that direction ever since.

My father. My thoughts continued to bounce back to him. Was he the only person in my life I could fully trust? He is probably already following the trail I made. He is probably on his way to come see me again.

I miss him. Especially after the whole ordeal with my companions. How would he even survive each challenge we were forced to face?

And what Oliver told me. I can't even begin to comprehend his words. Could I really trust him? I still do have outstanding questions when it comes to him too. Like, why spend an entire year in a random mysterious cabin with a clearly dangerous, murderous old man in the middle of the tunnels? That's weird. Why not try to head back to the Underground? Was Frank holding him captive there so he was too scared to escape? Oliver tried to cast doubt about June and Leo, and warned that they would betray me. Is that what happened to him? I have no idea if he was able to take two additional people with him, but how else would he know this to be an absolute truth? Maybe Oliver was right. After how Leo had acted, I wouldn't even be surprised. I don't truly know what he is capable of anymore. But June was different.

June. Sweet, loving June. How could she hurt someone? How could she hurt me, the person she has called her best friend? She wouldn't be able to do that! Not June...

Maybe that was just wishful thinking. Maybe I just didn't like the idea of losing her.

At that moment, Diamond flew directly in front of me, trying to get my attention. Where did she come from? I had forgotten completely about my newest friend! She continued to zoom down the tunnel as fast as light. I ran a full sprint to catch up to her, but I lost sight of her. It was like she had vanished into thin air. When I ran out of the tunnel to continue, I was in…a daycare? It was like magic, the walls of the tunnels vanished into this mysterious space.

It was just like the daycare in the Underground, but *colorful.* The daycare I went to when I was young had white walls, white floors, a white carpet, and white toys. But this one was littered with every color of the rainbow. It was so bright and happy and *perfect*. It is what every child would dream to have, and standing in the middle of the room, I appreciated the uniqueness of the colorful space. The walls had nature murals, brightly featuring landscapes and animals. The ceiling depicted a sunny sky with gorgeous puffy clouds.

I wish I could see the actual sky.

At that moment, I made a decision. If the other two did end up betraying me like Oliver forewarned, I would go into the Above and find all the answers to my questions. I would see everything that I had only ever experienced through books. I would see and explore it all.

I held my mother's necklace in my hand, and closed my eyes, promising myself this one last desire.

"Help protect me in my journey, mother. Keep me out of harm's way. I hope in the afterlife, you had a chance to see the stars. I love you."

After a few minutes of standing in silence, I realized that there was no actual door in this mysterious space. The tunnel led directly into this room, but there was only one way in and one way out. I was standing at another dead end. Everything about this was odd and out of place. I appreciated all of the ways it was different from the Underground, but part of me also knew that this was not the Above and I had not yet arrived.

I heard a tiny giggle and looked up to see Beth staring at me as she also entered the room.

"Who were you talking to?" she inquired.

"Oh, sometimes I talk to myself. I was thinking about my mother. She passed away when I was young, and talking aloud helps me get through hard times," I embarrassingly answered.

"I don't have a mother either. Father says I resemble her. Except for this," she said as she rested her palm on the side of her face, covering the discolored marking that wouldn't wash away.

"I think your marking makes you very unique and special. You should think of it that way," I assured her. She was pleased with this idea and smiled warmly.

"Do you know what this room is used for? It's so unusual." I asked her.

"Oh, this is my play area. My father built this for me when I was very young so that I would have a clean, safe space to spend time in. Isn't it lovely?" she asked while longingly looking over the room.

"It really is," I commented trying to piece all of her stories into the puzzle. I continued, "You know, it actually looks almost identical to a room I grew up in when I was also very young. The main difference is that my room was completely white. I like your room much better. The colors make it feel like it comes to life."

"That's so neat!" Beth chimed in, interrupting my train of thought. "I like coming here to read my books because the lighting is much better here."

I was about to agree with her when I heard footsteps approaching. I turned to see Leo and June standing in the doorframe of the strange, little daycare. I stared at them, and they stared right back.

"What is it?" I asked impatiently.

Leo, completely unphased by the room, or by Beth's presence, was the one to answer, "We found the entrance to the Above."

CHAPTER 29

They had found a staircase. It was a very, very large spiral staircase made of stone. I had tried my best to convince Beth to come with us, much to the dismay of my intrusive companions. She wouldn't budge. She insisted she had to stay because her father needed to know where she was at all times. I was forced to leave her behind, yet again. When we started the ascent up the stairs it seemed never ending. But we didn't dare stop. We took steady steps, peering upward around every bend. It took what felt like forever for us to reach the top, and when we finally arrived, we came face to face with a barrier that prevented us from moving forward. We came to an immediate stop. An enormous, rod iron gate obstructed our path. Its huge hinges were bracing the two massive doors on either side, and an incredibly large and solid lock secured the gates shut.

I reached for one of the knives in my pack. I tried using the smallest blade I had to pick the lock. In that small moment in time, it was silent apart from our breathing and the sound of metal against metal. Everything between me and my companions was awkward and strange. Part of me wished it wasn't. We weren't really talking to each other. We were just going through the motions, trying to reach a destination.

I got the gate open after a little while. None of us could believe what was on the other side.

It was a cave, just like all the other ones I had walked through along this route, but this one was littered with *crystals*. They were coming out of the floors, walls, and ceiling. They were hidden in every nook and cranny of the room. There were tiny crystals, and crystals larger than an entire person.

And they were *colorful*. There was a crystal for every color in the rainbow. There was red and orange, yellow and green, blue and purple, and pink with aquamarine. It was stunning. Absolutely stunning. Spotlights shone brightly on these colorful crystals.

In the center of the far back wall was a metal box. It was the only true break separating itself from the colorful surroundings. It was an elevator. I somehow knew that this elevator would transport me to the Above. Its existence in this very unusual cavern was odd, but what was even stranger was that there was no obvious button to call for the elevator.

The path to this elevator was very clear, as the floor had rows of slotted grooves carved out of the stone. I bent down to examine them more closely, and noticed that from left to right, the openings went from smallest to largest. There were 7 rows, each row containing 7 slots. As I began to stand back up, my eye caught a rectangular slab that was cemented into the floor directly in front of the elevator. Walking over and standing directly over it I read it aloud:

"From red to violet, align the crystal light.
Small to large, their spectrum bright,
shall awaken the path from dark to sight."

Well that was interesting. My two companions stood beside me looking at the slab themselves as I began to reread the passage over and over in my mind.

"What is this? What does it even mean?" June asked.

"I think it's a riddle we have to solve. I think it may be the only way to access the elevator." I replied.

Leo contemplated this and commented, "I don't even know what any of this means. How will we ever figure this out?"

I could tell they were beginning to feel anxious. I myself knew I had to figure this out or we'd be stuck in these tunnels forever. This was not an option. I refocused on the passage and worked it out line by line. *"From red to violet, align the crystal light."* I remembered the basics of colors from seeing illustrations in books depicting rainbows. Rainbows have seven primary colors, and they are red, orange, yellow, green, blue, indigo, and violet. That tracked. I then realized that the second part was an even bigger clue, *"Small to large, their spectrum bright,*

shall awaken the path from dark to sight." The path itself
was the key! Seven rows, seven slots. In a room full of
colorful crystals. I walked over and picked up a nearby
crystal in an attempt to test my theory. It was a small red
crystal and I carefully placed it into the slot nearest me.
The crystal began to faintly glow.

"Guys! I think I've figured it out! We need to gather
crystals of every color and fill in the rows in rainbow
order until we reach the elevator," I excitedly stated.

"What's a rainbow?" they asked, almost in unison.
Dumbfoundedly, I looked up to see both she and Leo
staring at me, still completely clueless as to how to help
or proceed. I tried my best to explain the concept of color
and as such, they tried their best to at least collect the
red crystals. Red came easier to them since it was the
closest color to the ruby in my necklace. After that their
attention drifted and I worked alone through the rest.

◆ ◆ ◆

I was tired of seeing crystals. Who knew it would
be so difficult to find 7 crystals of each color, in specific
sizes in a room full of colorful crystals.

When Leo and June just gave up and decided not
to help me complete the challenge they just sat together
watching me from the corner of the room. I did it all on
my own. For *hours.* But I did it.

As I successfully placed each crystal into the slot,
the glow amplified signifying it was placed correctly.

Row by row the light filled the cavern and illuminated into a prism of color. The colors refracted onto the elevator doors, creating that of an actual rainbow. It was beautiful. I carefully put the last remaining violet crystal into the one last remaining slot, and the challenge was completed.

The rainbow of colors illuminated the room so brightly it was as if I was transported into a magical realm. I looked up and all around me, just relishing in this special and rare experience. The door opened ever so silently. But there it was. The elevator was waiting for me.

Yes! Finally! After such a long time of being below, I would finally see the sky! I began to laugh, and I ran towards the elevator.

"We did it," I exclaimed, "We did it!"

"Julia." I heard my name bellowed out, tense and firm.

Leo. I had almost forgotten about him. About what Oliver told me.

As I turned around, I saw it. I saw it all flash before my eyes. He was pointing a gun at my head. Where did he get that from? I had never seen a gun in the Underground and didn't think they existed in our society. Has he been carrying this the entire time? Was the Counselor the one who supplied Leo with that weapon?

In front of me, Leo's face was stone cold. He wasn't showing an ounce of emotion. And June. Sweet June was by his side, with an expression I had never thought could be on her kind face. A grin. A horrible, cruel grin. Were these the people I once trusted? Were they the ones I once loved?

"Don't move, or I'll shoot you," Leo ordered.

It was strange how I felt completely helpless in this dire situation.

"Why?" I asked him, tears swelling up in my eyes, "Why are you doing this?"

"I got the order from the Counselor," he said, his words emotionless, "And I follow orders."

"Even orders to kill another person?" I asked, "I loved you, Leo. What happened?"

"I found out the truth about you," he responded, slowly lowering the gun as he divulged this news to me.

What could he mean by that? I never hid anything from anyone. Unless it was about the library, I don't have a clue what this could possibly be. But everyone knew the librarians didn't share their knowledge with anyone else. So it couldn't be that. What was it, then? Why am I a threat to the Counselor and the Underground?

"We were informed of something that would probably surprise you," June said, with both humor and cruelty in her smile, "We found out that you, Julia Brown, are a direct descendant from a citizen of the Above. They are our enemies, which means you are our enemy too."

I took a step back in shock. Leo tensed up and again raised the gun, pointing it squarely at me, causing me to freeze in place.

I gripped my mother's necklace. The entire reason I had never met her...was because she was from the Above.

"That mother of yours was from the Above," June explained, acknowledging the necklace, "She was meant to be a spy for the Counselor, but she betrayed our society. She tried to escape, taking you with her, but she failed. They searched the tunnels, looking for her, but they found you instead. A young child left alone, wearing her traitor mother's ruby necklace."

June paused, and then added, "She was found dead in a different part of the tunnels the very next day."

My mother had wanted to take me to see the sky. But she had failed. At that moment, I made a promise to her.

I promise to see the stars, mother. I promise.

June kept talking. She kept saying things about how I would betray the Underground too, and how they needed to get rid of anything that could harm them.

Why was the Above even an enemy of the Underground! In every book I had ever read describing the people of the Above, they had always seemed like these incredible people. Sure, there were some bad people out in this world, but that's not everyone. I believed in a world where people could all exist in peace. They're not all horrible.

As June's voice continued to drone on, I was slowly

backing away from them, making my way closer and closer to the opened elevator. Diamond flew into the cavern from out of nowhere and began fluttering in front of me, as if to protect me and act as a barrier between me and them.

A loud shot rang out. I fell to my knees, and closed my tear-filled eyes. Had Diamond managed to throw off Leo's aim? I was expecting to feel pain in my chest or my head. But instead, I felt it in my leg.

Did Leo actually miss his target because of Diamond, or did he have some part of him that still cared for me? I could not accept that he was without a bit of emotion left in him.

I felt someone push me into the metal box, and I saw Diamond fly in as well, circling above my head, just as the elevator doors shut. That good bird. I knew I could trust her.

Holding my mother's necklace, I felt the elevator begin to rise. It was taking me to the land my mother loved. To the place I was born to be.

The world around me started to get blurry. I kept slipping in and out of consciousness, seeing hazy images of blue shifting side to side above me. It took a long time to make it all the way up. Why was the Underground so far beneath the ground? Who made that decision?

My own blood surrounded the area around me. I was gonna bleed out. I was gonna die here.

Then the doors opened. There was a rush of people

and movement and *color.* That bittersweet color. I longed to live in it. I was so close, yet drifting so far away.

The subtle scent of vanilla became increasingly stronger as I was gently lifted from the floor. I struggled to open my eyes, just enough to see the Head Librarian's face seriously looking forward, forward as he rushed me into the Above.

As I slipped into the land of sleep, I knew it would be okay. I did it.

I made it to the world Above.

EPILOGUE

"Is she dead?" the Counselor asked, sitting at his desk. It was located in a small room, which was accessed from a long, narrow hallway.

"We have no idea," the other young man in the room said, "She fell into the elevator at the last second after I shot her."

"You're the one who missed and shot her in the leg, Leo," the young woman named June added in, "We are so sorry, sir. We understand if you are disappointed with our work."

"It's alright," the Counselor replied, "We'll have another opportunity in the future. Was there anything else that could help us locate her?"

"Well," June answered, "There was this creature that followed her around. Leo has one of its droppings."

The young man handed the Counselor a bright blue object. The Counselor examining it announced, "It's a feather. A feather, belonging to either a parrot or a macaw."

He then stood up from his chair, resting his hands on the desk in front of him. He let out a long sigh. "Did you at least remember the route? Do you know how to reach the entrance to the Above?"

It was the first time the teenagers witnessed the Counselor lose his composure. Both teens looked at each other and then back to the Counselor and shook their heads "no" in unison.

"The two of you will not have to participate in this ordeal until I call on you again, if I call on you at all," he corrected and then continued, "You have played your roles reasonably well, and I, personally, believe it won't be too difficult to retrace your route, or apprehend her. You are excused."

"Thank you, Counselor," said Leo.

"Thank you, Counselor," said June, as they both stood up and exited the room.

The leader of the Underground was now alone, at a desk, in a small room that was accessed from a long, narrow hallway, in an underground society, and he was holding a feather. A feather that was linked to the person he wanted dead.

◆ ◆ ◆

"When will she be awake?" a male voice asked. I could hear and feel everything around me, but I still couldn't move or see.

"She is in a coma," another male said, "I've told you this a million times already, you idiot."

"Yea, but that doesn't answer my question," male number one said, "When will she be out of the coma?"

"There are approximately three days before she wakes up," a female voice answered.

The first male just snickered, "Nerd."

"At least she has a brain," male number two retorted.

"Hey!" male number one exclaimed, "That's mean! I'm not that dumb!"

"Yea, sure," the woman answered. The three of them continued to joke and argue and talk above me. But I could only think of one thing.

"Where the hell am I?"

Acknowledgments

I want to thank my parents who have guided me through this journey. Thank you for becoming my editors and spending the time to iron out every little detail in this novel. You embraced the journey, my story, and me. I will be forever grateful.

I want to especially thank my mom. Thank you for helping me develop the Head Librarian character. Having your perspective and knowledge of the adult challenges he may have faced was beyond helpful. This book would not be the same without you and your support.

Thank you to my grandmother, who is always there for me, encouraging my story writing and being my biggest champion.

Thank you to my middle school teachers, who encourage and support my passion for learning, reading, and writing. I am so lucky to be surrounded by such amazing people everyday.

Thank you to my incredible friends, who were entirely supportive of this book from beginning to end.

And finally, thank you, dear reader, for coming along this journey with me through The World Below.

About The Author

Natalie L. Morris is a middle school student from California. She lives with her parents, grandmother, and three dogs. She enjoys reading, painting, playing guitar, and song writing. This novel, "The World Below", is her first ever published book. But don't worry! There's much more to come in the future! She invites you to visit her online at www.natmotime.com.

Made in the USA
Las Vegas, NV
20 November 2024